THE ADORATION OF
JENNA FOX

Praise for **The Adoration of Jenna Fox**:

'Outstanding examination of identity, science and ethics…
Pearson reveals the truth layer by layer, maintaining taut suspense
and psychological realism as she probes philosophical notions of
personhood.' *Kirkus Reviews*, starred review

'Pearson raises the ante in unexpected ways until the very last
page…' *Publishers Weekly*, starred review

'This is a beautiful blend of science fiction, medical thriller, and teen-
relationship novel that melds into a seamless whole that will please
fans of all three genres.' *School Library Journal*, starred review

'This novel is truly unlike any other I have ever read and is a breath
of fresh air in the often predictable world of teen literature.' *ELLEgirl*

'This provocative exploration of bio-ethics is heightened by the
portrait of a family under enormous stress and the subtle thematic
threads of faith and science woven through the story, making this
a thriller with uncharacteristic literary merit.' *The Horn Book
Magazine*

'This is an amazingly powerful, thought-provoking, just brilliant
novel.' *Teen Book Review*

THE ADORATION OF JENNA FOX

MARY E PEARSON

WALKER BOOKS

First published in Great Britain 2010 by Walker Books Ltd
87 Vauxhall Walk, London SE11 5HJ

2 4 6 8 10 9 7 5 3

This book has been typeset in Garamond and News Gothic
Printed and bound in Great Britain by Clays Ltd, St Ives plc

British Library Cataloguing in Publication Data:
a catalogue record for this book is available from the British Library

ISBN 978-1-4063-2301-6

www.walker.co.uk

For my wonderful husband, Dennis,
and my precious children, Jessica, Karen, and Ben

California

I used to be someone.

Someone named Jenna Fox.

That's what they tell me. But I am more than a name. More than they tell me. More than the facts and statistics they fill me with. More than the video clips they make me watch.

More. But I'm not sure what.

'Jenna, come sit over here. You don't want to miss this.' The woman I am supposed to call Mother pats the cushion next to her. 'Come,' she says again.

I do.

'This is an historic moment,' she says. She puts her arm around me and squeezes. I lift the corner of my mouth. Then the other: a smile. Because I know I am supposed to. It is what she wants.

'It's a first,' she says. 'We've never had a woman president of Nigerian descent before.'

'A first,' I say. I watch the monitor. I watch Mother's face. I've only just learned how to smile. I don't know how to match her other expressions. I should.

'Mom, come sit with us,' she calls out toward the kitchen. 'It's about to start.'

I know she won't come. She doesn't like me. I don't know how I know. Her face is as plain and expressionless to me as everyone else's. It is not her face. It is something else.

'I'm doing a few dishes. I'll watch from the monitor in here,' she calls back.

I stand. 'I can leave, Lily,' I offer.

She comes and stands in the arched doorway. She looks at Mother. They exchange an expression I try to understand. Mother's face drops into her hands. 'She's your nana, Jenna. You've always called her Nana.'

'That's all right. She can call me Lily,' she says and sits down on the other side of Mother.

Awareness

There is a dark place.

A place where I have no eyes, no mouth. No words.

I can't cry out because I have no breath. The silence is so
deep I want to die.

But I can't.

The darkness and silence go on forever.

It is not a dream.

I don't dream.

Waking

The accident was over a year ago. I've been awake for two weeks. Over a year has vanished. I've gone from sixteen to seventeen. A second woman has been elected president. A twelfth planet has been named in the solar system. The last wild polar bear has died. Headline news that couldn't stir me. I slept through it all.

I cried on waking. That's what they tell me. I don't remember the first day. Later I heard Lily whisper to Mother in the kitchen that my cries frightened her. 'It sounds like an animal,' she said.

I still cry on waking. I'm not sure why. I feel nothing. Nothing I can name, anyway. It's like breathing—something that happens over which I have no control. Father was here for my waking. He called it a beginning. He said it was good. I think he may have thought that anything I did was good. The first few days were difficult. My mind and body thrashed out of control. My mind settled first. They kept my arms strapped. By the second day my arms had settled, too. The house seemed busy. They checked me, probed, checked again and again, Father scanning my symptoms into the Netbook several times a day, someone relaying back treatment. But there was no treatment that I could see. Each day I improved. That was it. One day I couldn't walk. The next day I could. One day my right eyelid drooped. The next it didn't. One day my tongue lay like a lump of meat in my mouth, the next day it was articulating words that hadn't been spoken in over a year.

On the fifth day, when I walked out onto the veranda without stumbling, Mother cried and said, 'It's a miracle. An absolute miracle.'

'Her gait is still not natural. Can't you see that?' Lily said.

Mother didn't answer.

On the eighth day Father had to return to work in Boston. He and Mother whispered, but I still heard. *Risky...have to get back...you'll be fine.* Before he left he cupped my face in both of his hands. 'Little by little, Angel,' he said. 'Be patient. Everything will come back. Over time all the connections will be made.' I think my gait is normal now. My memory is not. I don't remember my mother, my father, or Lily. I don't remember that I once lived in Boston. I don't remember the accident. I don't remember Jenna Fox.

Father says it will come in time. 'Time heals,' he says.

I don't tell him that I don't know what time is.

Time

There are words.
Words I don't remember.
Not obscure words that I wouldn't be expected to know.
But simple ones.
Jump. Hot. Apple.
Time.
I look them up. I will never forget them again.
Where did those words go,
 those words that were once in my head?

Order

Curious adj. *1. Eager to learn or to know, inquisitive.*
2. Prying or meddlesome. 3. Inexplicable, highly unusual,
odd, strange.

The first week, Mother pored over the details of my life. My name. Childhood pets. Favorite books. Family vacations. And after each scene she described, she would ask, 'Remember?' Each time I said no, I saw her eyes change. They seemed to get smaller. Is that possible? I tried to say the nos more softly. I tried to make each one sound different than the one before. But on Day Six her voice cracked as she told me about my last ballet recital. *Remember?*

On Day Seven, Mother handed me a small box. 'I don't want to pressure you,' she said. 'They're in order. Mostly all labeled. Maybe watching them will help bring things back.' She hugged me. I felt her fuzzy sweater. I felt the coolness of her cheek. Things I can feel. Hard. Soft. Rough. Smooth. But the inside kind of feel, it is all the same, like foggy mush. Is that the part of me that is still asleep? I had moved my arms around her and tried to mimic her squeeze. She seemed pleased. 'I love you, Jenna,' she said. 'Anything you want to ask me, I'm here. I want you to know that.'

Thank you was the right response, so I said it. I don't know if that was something I remembered or something I had just learned. I don't love her. I sensed that I should, but how can you love someone you don't know? But I did feel something in that foggy mush. Devotion? Obligation? I wanted her to be pleased. I thought about her offer, *anything you want to ask me.* I had nothing to ask. The questions hadn't come yet.

So I watched the first disc. It seemed logical to go in order. It was of me in utero. *Hours* of me in utero. I was the first, I learned. There had been two boy babies before me, but they didn't live past the first trimester. With me, Mother and Father took extra measures, and they worked. I was the one and only. Their miracle child. I watched the fetus that was me, floating in a dark watery world, and wondered if I should remember that, too.

Each day I watch more discs, trying to regain who I was. Some are stills, some are movies. There are dozens of the two-inch discs. Maybe a hundred. Thousands of hours of me.

I settle on the large sofa. Today I watch Year Three / Jenna Fox. It begins with my third birthday party. A small girl runs, laughing at nothing at all, and is finally stopped by a tall, weathered stone wall. She slaps tiny starburst hands against the stone and looks back at the camera. I pause the scene. I scan the smile. The face. She has something. Something I don't see in my own face, but I don't know what it is. Maybe just a word I have lost? Maybe more. I scan the large rough stones her hands rest against. It is the small enclosed garden of the brownstone where we once lived. I remember it from yesterday on Disc Eighteen.

'Play,' I say, and the scene moves forward. I watch the golden-haired girl squeal and run and hide her face between two trousered legs. Then the three-year-old is scooped upside down into the air and the view zooms up to Father's face laughing and nuzzling into her belly. My belly. The three-year-old laughs. She seems to like it. I walk over to the mirror that hangs near the bookcase. I am seventeen now, but I see a resemblance. Same blond hair. Same blue eyes. But the teeth are different. Three-year-old teeth are so small. My fingers. My hands. All much larger now. Almost a whole different person. And yet that is *me*. At least that is what they say. I return to watch the rest of the party, the bath time, the ballet lesson, the finger painting, the temper tantrum, the story time, the everything of three-year-old Jenna Fox's life that mattered to Mother and Father.

I hear footsteps behind me. I don't turn. They are Lily's. Her feet make a different sound on the floor than Mother's. Movement is crisp, distinct. I hear every nuance. Was I always this sensitive to sound? She stands somewhere behind me. I wait for her to speak. She doesn't. I'm not sure what she wants.

'You don't have to watch them in order, you know,' she finally says.

'I know. Mother told me.'

'There are discs of when you were a teenager.'

'I still am a teenager.'

There is a pause. A deliberate pause, I suspect. 'I suppose,' she says. She comes around so she is in my vision. 'Aren't you curious?'

Curious. It's a word I looked up this morning after Mother used it to describe Mr Bender who lives behind us on the other side of the pond. I don't know if Lily is asking me if I am inquisitive or odd.

'I've been in a coma for over a year. I guess that makes me highly unusual; odd; and strange. Yes, Lily. I am curious.'

Lily's arms unfold and slide to her sides. Her head tilts slightly. She's a pretty woman. She looks to be fifty when I know she must be at least sixty. Small wrinkles deepen around her eyes. The subtleties of expression still escape me.

'You should watch them out of order. Skip straight to the last year.'

Lily leaves the room, and on Day Fifteen of being awake, I make my first independent decision. I will watch the discs in order.

Widening

There is something curious about where we live. Something curious about Lily. Something curious about Father and his nightly phone calls with Mother. And certainly something curious about me. Why can I remember the details of the French Revolution but I can't remember if I ever had a best friend?

Day Sixteen

When I woke this morning, I had questions. I wondered where they had all been hiding. *Time heals.* Is this what Father meant? Or were the words that had been lost in my head simply trying to find the proper order? Besides questions, the word *careful* came to mind, too. Why? I'm beginning to think I must trust words when they come to me.

'Jenna, I'm leaving,' Mother calls from the front step. 'Are you sure you'll be okay?'

Mother is going to town. It is the first time I have seen her leave the house since Day One.

'I'll be fine,' I tell her. 'My nutrients are on the counter. I know how much to take.' I can't eat regular food yet. When I asked them why, they stumbled over each other's words trying to explain. They finally said that after a year of being fed through a tube, my system can't utilize regular food for a while. I never saw the tube. Maybe that's what's on the last disc that Lily told me to watch. Why would she want me to see that?

'Don't leave the house,' Mother adds.

'She won't,' Lily answers.

Mother is going to town to interview workmen. She is a certified restoration consultant. Or was. She had a business in Boston restoring brownstones. It was her specialization. She was busy. Everyone wants to restore everything. Old is in demand. Lily says she had a respected reputation. Her career is over now because of me. There are no brownstones in California. But Mother says the Cotswold cottage we live in needs lots of restoration, and now that I am feeling better, it's time she began making it livable. One restoration is not that different from another, she says. Fixing me and the Cotswold are her new careers.

She is halfway down the narrow front walk when I ask her my first question. I know it's not a good time for her.

'Mother, why did we move here?'

She stops. I think I see a slight stumble. She turns around. Her eyes are wide. She doesn't speak, so I continue. 'When the doctors, Father, and your career are all in Boston, why are we *here*?'

Mother looks down for a moment so I can't see her face, then looks up again. She smiles. One corner. Then the other. A careful smile. 'There are lots of reasons, Jenna. I can't discuss them all right now or I'll miss the shuttle into town, but the main reason is that we thought it would be best for you to have a quiet place to recover. And our plan seems to be working, doesn't it?'

Smooth. Practiced. I can hear it in the singsong of her voice. In some ways it's almost reasonable, but I can see the holes. Having a quiet place is not as important as being close to doctors. But

I nod. There is something about her eyes. Eyes don't breathe. I know that much. But hers look breathless.

My Room

I go to my room. I don't want to. But before she left, Mother made one last request. 'Go to your room, Jenna. I think you might need some rest.' I don't need rest, and I don't want to go, but before I know it, my feet are taking me up the stairs and I am closing my door behind me. I know it would please her.

My room is on the second floor—one of ten rooms on the upper level, along with an assortment of closets, bathrooms, nooks, and other small windowless rooms that seem to have no purpose. Mine is the only one that is clean and has furniture. The others are empty except for an occasional spider or a piece of trash left by the previous occupants. The lower floor has at least another ten rooms, and only half of those rooms are furnished. A few of the rooms are locked. I have not seen them. Mother and Lily have rooms down there. The cottage is not a cottage at all. I looked it up to be sure. I looked up *Cotswold*, too. It's a sheep. So we should live in a one-room house meant for sheep. I haven't seen any sheep here either.

My room is at the end of a long hallway. It is the largest room on the upper level, which makes the lone bed, desk, and chair seem small and awkward. The polished-wood floor reflects the pieces of furniture. It is a cold room. Not in temperature, but in temperament. It reflects nothing of the person who inhabits it. Or maybe it does.

The only color in the room is the custard-yellow coverlet on the bed. The desktop is clear except for the Netbook that Father used to communicate with the doctors. No papers. No books. No clutter. Nothing.

The bedroom opens into a large arched dressing room that connects with a closet that connects with another smaller closet that has a small door at the back, which I can't open. It is an odd zigzag tunneling arrangement. Was my room in Boston like this? Four shirts and four pairs of pants hang in the first closet. All of them are blue. Below them are two pairs of shoes. Nothing is in the second closet. I run my hands along the walls and wonder at the emptiness.

I look out my window. Across our yard and the pond, I see curious Mr Bender, a mere speck in the distance. He appears to be squatting, looking at something on the ground. He moves a few steps forward and disappears from view, hidden by the edge of a eucalyptus grove that borders both our properties. I turn back to my room.

A wooden chair.

A bare desk.

A plain bed.

So little. Is this all Jenna Fox adds up to?

A Question I Will Never Ask Mother:

Did I have friends?

I was sick for over a year and yet there is not a single card, letter,
   balloon, or wilted bouquet of flowers in my room.

The Netbook never buzzes for me.

Not even an old classmate's simple inquiry.

I may not remember everything, but I know there should be
   these things.

Something.

I know when someone is sick that people check on her.

What kind of person was Jenna Fox that she didn't have any
   friends?

Was she someone I even want to remember?

Everyone should have at least one friend.

More

I hear Lily humming. My feet fumble like they have a will of their own, but I try to control them so she won't hear me. I lean close to the wall and peek into the kitchen. Her back is to me. She spends most of her time in the kitchen preparing elaborate dishes. She used to be chief of internal medicine at Boston University Hospital. Father was a resident under her. That is how he met Mother. Lily gave it up. I don't know why. Now her passions are gardening and cooking. It seems that everyone in this house is reinventing themselves and no one is who they once were.

When she is not in the kitchen cooking, she is out in the greenhouse getting it in order. I can't eat her foods, and I wonder if that is part of the reason she doesn't like me. She clanks pots and then turns on the faucet. I make my move for the front door.

The hinges on the heavy wooden door squeak when I exit, but she doesn't follow. The sound blends with the clanking pots and rushing water. I have been no farther than the front steps of the house, except for once when it was dark and Mother took me for a short walk to Lily's greenhouse. Mother told me from the start that I must stay close. She is afraid I will get lost.

> **Lost** adj. *1. No longer known. 2. Unable to find the way.*
> *3. Ruined or destroyed.*

I'm afraid I already am.

The noon sun is bright. It hurts my eyes. I ease the door shut so Lily won't hear, and I hurry across the lawn. I won't go far.

I will keep the house in sight. *Careful.* The word comes again, like a hedge in front of me, but pushing from behind, too. I pass the chimney of the fireplace in the living room. Its top bricks have tumbled to the ground and weeds almost obscure them. Bright green lichens creep up the remaining bricks. I walk around the far side of the garage so Lily won't see me. Several of the windows are boarded up, and a whole section of shingles is missing from the roof. Money doesn't seem to be a problem for Mother. I wonder why, in over a year of my being in a coma, she didn't have time to make the barest of repairs.

Once I am past the garage, I have a clear view of curious Mr Bender's property, but I don't see him. Our backyard slopes down gently toward a large pond. Its waters are still. The pond separates our yard from Mr Bender's, and the small creek that feeds it separates our neighbors' yards to the south, like a natural curving fence. To the north, where the pond overflows, the creek continues, disappearing into a forest of eucalyptus.

A few more steps and I see Mr Bender, sitting on his haunches, like I have seen three-year-old Jenna sit in the video discs. It is an odd stance for a grown man. He clutches something in one hand and stretches out his other to something on the ground. He is so still, it stops me.

Curious. Odd. Strange. Mother was right about him.

I walk farther down the slope until I am stopped by the pond. I start toward the forest. The trees are spindly but numerous, and only a few yards in, the pond stops and spills into the creek. The flow is barely stronger than Lily's kitchen faucet and only a few inches deep at most. I step on dry stones that rise above the trickle to get across to the other side, and I walk up the slope of

Mr Bender's yard. I should be afraid. Mother would want me to be afraid. But other than Mother, Father, and Lily, Mr Bender is the only human being I've seen since I woke up. I want to speak to someone who doesn't know me. Someone who doesn't know Lily or Mother. Someone outside our own curious circle. He sees me coming and rises off his haunches. He is tall, much larger than I thought. I stop.

'Hello,' he calls.

I don't move.

'Lost?' he says.

I look back at my house. I look at my hands. I turn them over and examine both sides. My name is Jenna Fox. 'No,' I answer. I step forward.

He holds out his hand. 'I'm Clayton Bender. You the new neighbor?' He nods toward our house.

New? What is new to him? Is a year new? 'I'm Jenna Fox. Yes, I live over there.' I reach my hand out to him and we shake.

'Your hands are like ice, young lady. You still acclimating?'

I don't know what that means, but I nod and say yes. 'I saw you from my room. I saw you squatting. You're curious.'

He laughs and says, 'You mean you're curious.'

'My grandmother thinks so.'

He laughs again and shakes his head. I wonder if laughing is another curious thing about him. 'Well, Jenna, you saw me squatting because I was working on this. Come take a look.' He turns and walks a few feet away and points to the ground. I follow.

'What is it?' I ask.

'I haven't named it yet, but I think it will be *Pine Serpent.* Maybe not. I'm an environmental artist.'

'A what?'

'I create art from found objects in nature.'

I look at the hundreds of long pine needles, each perfectly aligned with the next, each end carefully pushed into the loose soil, forming a curved snake that flows in and out of the ground. I want to reach down and stroke it, but I know that would destroy it. I don't see the point. He has spent all morning creating something that will be blown away or trampled by tomorrow. 'Why?' I ask.

He laughs again. Why does he do that? He is more curious than I am. 'You're a tough critic, Jenna Fox. I create art because I need to. It's just something in me. Like breathing.'

How can a pine serpent be in him? Especially one that will not last. 'This will be gone by tomorrow.'

'Yes, it probably will. That's the beauty of it and what makes it even more wondrous. At least to me. It's delicate, temporal, but eternal, too. It will go back into the environment to be used again and again, in nature's canvas. I just rearrange parts of nature for a short time so people will notice the beauty of what they usually ignore. So they'll stop and—'

'But no one will see it here.'

'I take photos when I'm done, Jenna. I'm not that temporal. I have to eat, too. You've never heard the name Clayton Bender?'

'No.'

He smiles. 'Well, I suppose some of my work's not well known, but early in my career I created an icicle sculpture in the snow. *White on White.* That one made my career. It's hard to go into an office building or doctor's office without seeing it. Not my best, but the best known. White goes with everything,

I guess. That's what mostly paid for this place. I sure couldn't afford it now.'

'Your house cost a lot?'

'All these do. You can't get houses like the ones in this neighborhood without a small fortune these days. But I got mine for next to nothing right after the big quake. You're too young to remember but—'

'Fifteen years ago. Southern California. Nineteen thousand people died. Two whole communities vanished into the ocean, and all major transportation systems were crippled as well as water flow to the southern half of the state. It was the greatest natural disaster our country has ever seen and, along with the Aureus epidemic that followed three months later, was considered the triggering event for the Second Great Depression, which lasted six years.'

I'm stunned. Is that the word? Yes, *stunned*. I don't know where all the facts came from.

Mr Bender draws in his breath. 'Well! You know your facts, don't you, Jenna? You a history buff?'

Was I? Am I? I am still absorbing how easily the facts flowed out of me. 'I must be.'

'Well, you got your facts straight. I got this house dirt cheap, because of all those terrible things. But now everyone's forgotten about the earthquake and the scientists say it'll be a few hundred years before we have another nine-pointer, so the prices have gone back through the roof.'

'Ours is in bad shape. I don't think it could be worth much.'

'It's been empty for years, but it won't take much to get it fixed up. I'm glad to see someone finally in it. When I saw you all moving in a couple of weeks ago, I was happy to see the place finally filled with a family.'

'Two weeks ago? We've been here longer than that.'

Mr Bender's brows dip. 'Of course. Yes, you must be right. I lose track of time,' he says.

But I sense he doesn't believe me. Maybe he doesn't want to argue. Neither do I.

'Are you going to take a picture?' I point to *Pine Serpent*.

'Not yet. I need to wait for the sun to get a little lower. And if I get lucky, I'm going to coax a few birds to pose with it. A modern-day lion-and-lamb thing.'

'You have birds?'

'Here. I'll show you. Over this way.'

He walks the slope toward an overgrown garden. Broken slabs of flagstone create a winding pathway through sprays of lavender, untamed boxwood, and lacy umbrellas of anise. A short distance in, the garden opens into a circular grassy area with a hewn-log bench at its center. Mr Bender sits and reaches beneath his seat for a small covered bowl. He scoops something into his palm. 'Sit,' he says. I do.

He holds his palm out, and instantly there are multiple chirps around us. 'Hold still,' he instructs. A small gray bird swoops over his palm without taking anything. Another one dives, hovers, and disappears like the other. Mr Bender doesn't move. Still another one swoops, flutters, and then lands on his wrist. It pecks a seed and flies away. Within moments two more land on his hand and greedily peck at the seed, braver than the rest. I am mesmerized by their perfect tiny beaks, their creamy clawed feet, and their layered gray feathers that fold together like a beautiful silk fan. I reach out to touch one, and they both skitter away.

'You have to be patient. Here, try it,' he says. He hands me the tub of seed, and I scoop out a handful. I put my palm out and wait. They chirp from the nearby jacaranda but don't budge from their perches. I thrust my palm out farther. We wait and are silent. I am careful not to move. I *am* patient.

They don't come.

'Maybe they're full,' Mr Bender says. 'You come back anytime, Jenna, and give it another try.'

I wonder. Anytime? The expressions that have blended together since I came out of my coma are beginning to emerge into patterns. Most of it centers in the eyes. Without words, the lids shape sounds. They speak different things just by the faintest of angles. It is coming to me now, the expression on Lily's face yesterday. Pain. And now, today, on Mr Bender's face, truth. He really does want me to come back. How can eyes speak so much? It is another thing that I find curious.

'I will,' I tell him. He stands and throws his few remaining seeds into the boxwood. A ruckus of chirps follows. They weren't full.

'I have to get back to work now, Jenna, but I do thank you for coming by.' We walk back down the pathway, but he stops at the garden edge and rubs the back of his neck. 'Be careful about where you wander, though. We've had a few incidents around here. Broken windows. Pets gone missing. And some other things. Most of the neighbors are friendly enough, but some, well, you never know.'

'And you do?'

'Let's just say there's not a thing you can't find on the Net, and I've made it a point to know my neighbors.' He looks off in the distance at a white house at the end of our lane.

'Thank you, Mr Bender. *Careful* is a word I pay attention to.'

Known

I have a friend. It changes everything. He may not be the normal sort of friend for a seventeen-year-old, but I am not normal either. For now, normal doesn't matter.

I don't know if I will ever remember Jenna. The Jenna I was, at least. Father seems to think I will. Mother desperately wants me to. But letting go of something old and building something new that is all my own feels good. I want more of this feeling.

I smile and I don't even have to think about lifting the corners of my mouth. It happens on its own. Mr Bender is curious. So am I. I'm not lost. I am no longer not known. Mr Bender knows me.

I can see our house as I make my way back down Mr Bender's slope. I walk into the eucalyptus grove to where the pond is dammed with earth and a weave of gnarled tree roots. I step on the first stone that rises above the trickling creek, but then something catches my eye. A white shimmer. The glare off the pond. It shoots up at me. Blinds me. Pulls me into it.

My foot slips from the rock into the creek. I hear noise.

Screams.

I feel myself fall, but I can't see where I am falling to. The world spins. My mouth opens. Screams. My hands thrash. Water pours in.

My nose. My mouth. Blackness. Gulps. Pain in my chest.

The pond is everywhere.

'Na! Na!' I feel rocks cutting into my knees. Glimmers.

Flashes. Beams of muted light. Syrupy sound. Down, down. Wet blackness covers me while glistening air bubbles rise above me.

'Jenna!'

I feel hands around my wrists. Hands shaking my shoulders.

'Jenna!'

I see Lily looking into my face. Lily pulling me to my feet.

'Jenna! What's the matter! What happened? Jenna! Jenna!'

The pond is still. My clothes are dry. One knee is cut. A small bead of watery blood forms. 'I—'

'Are you all right?' Lily's pupils are pinpoints. Her voice pierces me.

'I think so.' I'm not sure what happened. Everything seemed different. The pond was so huge, and I was so small. I thought it was covering me. I couldn't see.

I thought I was drowning.

Remembering

Mother signs off the Net with Father and crosses the kitchen to where I sit. She has been talking to him privately for fifteen minutes about the small cut on my knee. She tried to get Lily to treat it, but Lily balked, saying she hadn't practiced medicine in fifteen years and that she had never practiced *that* kind of medicine. 'He said it should be fine,' Mother says. 'It should heal just like any other cut.'

'It *is* just like any other cut.'

'Not exactly,' Lily mumbles as she sits in the chair opposite me.

Mother explodes. 'I told you, Jenna! I told you! I said don't leave the house!'

'But I did.'

Mother crumples into another chair at the table. She rubs one temple. 'What happened?' she says more softly.

'I was crossing the creek. I stepped on the first stone. And then...' I try to remember exactly what happened next.

'Then *what?*' Mother says, her voice wrung tight.

I remember. More. 'Did I almost drown?'

'The creek's only a few inches—'

Lily cuts her off. 'Yes. A long time ago. She wasn't even two.'

'But she couldn't possibly remember—'

'I remember.'

I remember. I look at Mother and Lily, their expressions identical, like the air has been squeezed from their lungs. 'I remember birds. White birds. I remember falling. I fell so far. And I screamed and water filled my mouth...'

Lily pushes back her chair and stands. 'We were at the bay. I let go of Jenna's hand for only a second, just long enough to get money out of my purse for a snow cone. I was paying for it, and when I turned around, she was already at the end of the dock. She ran so fast. It was the gulls. There were gulls at the end of the dock and she didn't stop. She was so focused on those birds, she didn't hear me scream. I saw her go over and I ran. She was already sinking, and I jumped in after her.'

Lily talks about me like she is talking about someone else.

Like I am not in the room.

'You bought me another snow cone. A week later when we went back. It was—'

'Cherry.'

Mother begins to sob. She scoots her chair back and comes to me. Her arms wrap around my shoulders and she kisses my cheek, my hair. 'You're remembering, Jenna. Just like your father said. This is just the beginning.'

Remembering.

Jenna Fox is inside me after all. Just when I was ready to move on without her, she surfaces. *Don't forget me,* she says.

I don't think she'll let me.

Visitors

Kara.

And Locke, too.

They come to me. Mother and Father are right. Bits. Pieces. More. It comes back. These pieces wind through the night. Faces that wake me. I sit up, hot, afraid.

I had friends. Kara and Locke. But I don't remember when. Or where. School? The neighborhood? I can't remember where we went or what we did. But I see their faces. Looming close in front of mine, breathless.

I knew them. *I knew them deeply.* Where are they now?

I sit in my bed, in the dark, listening to the midnight creaks of our house, trying to conjure more than their faces, trying to push them into rooms, desks, and voices that will trigger more. But only their faces, close, eye to eye, are revealed. They linger before me like they have found my scent.

Tell me. Tell me who you are.

Tell me who I am.

Timing

Lily slides the garage door up. It screeches and shudders from lack of use until it finally completes its noisy path. Inside the dark cavern is an old pink hybrid wedged between stacks of boxes.

'I'll back it out, and then you can get in.' Her voice is sharp. 'And don't tell your mother. I'll catch it if she finds out I took you out in public.'

'I'd rather stay home.'

'I'd rather you stayed home, too. But I have errands to run, and I'm not taking a chance on you gallivanting off again.'

'I wouldn't.' *Gallivanting?*

Lily grunts. She squeezes between stacks of boxes and backs the car out, and I get in beside her. 'Are we going to take the T?'

Lily brakes. 'You remember the T?'

I am annoyed with everyone asking what I do and don't remember. It's all a matter of degrees. Do I remember riding somewhere on the T? Having somewhere important to go? Riding with someone who mattered to me? No. Do I remember what it looks like and what it does? Yes. I give the best response I can. A shrug.

'Well, this isn't Boston, and there is no T. And the shuttle doesn't go where we need going so I'm driving the whole way. Problem with that?'

I don't answer.

She puts the car in gear and lurches forward, passing the houses on our lane. There are only five. The others are not Cotswold cottages. Each one is different. An English Tudor right next door, then a large Old Mission style estate; next a sprawling Crafts-man, and last, the white house that Mr Bender paired with the word *careful*. It is a massive Georgian with tall, white pillars at the entrance. I am amused that I know the styles. But I am sure in Mother's office there are volumes and volumes on architecture. Maybe the old Jenna read them.

Mr Bender said the homes in this neighborhood cost a fortune. Looking at these, I believe him. We also still have the brownstone in Boston, which I am sure costs a fortune as well. 'Are Mother and Father rich?' I ask.

'That's an odd question.'

'I'm odd. Remember?'

'Yes. Pretty much filthy.'

'Rich, you mean?'

'That's what I said.'

'From restoring brownstones?'

Lily laughs.

'So it's Father then. Doctors make that much?'

'No.'

I see her hesitate. The car idles at the stop sign. She sighs like she is giving up something precious and I had better appreciate it. 'He started his own biotech company and sold it four years ago. That's where he made his money. He developed Bio Gel. It changed everything as far as transplants were concerned. Instead of just a few hours, organs could be shelved indefinitely waiting for the right recipient. He was on the news and made a big splash. Anything else?'

'If he sold his company, where does he work now?'

'Same place.'

I don't understand, but Lily isn't offering any further explanation and I am tired of prying information out of her. I change the subject and gesture back to the street we have just exited. 'Do you know the neighbors?' I ask.

'Not yet,' Lily answers. Again, she doesn't elaborate. I know she'd rather enjoy the silence. I don't think that will happen.

'You've been here for over a year. Why haven't you met them?'

'What makes you think we've been here that long?'

'Mother said we moved here because—'

'We've been here two and a half weeks.'

'That's impossible,' I say. 'That's almost exactly how long I've been awake. We move here one day and I wake up the next? What are the chances...'

I don't say any more. Neither does Lily. I remember Mr Bender's comment about us only being here for two weeks, too. It's true. How could Mother and Father have known? After I spent over a year in a coma, how could they have predicted exactly when I would wake up and then move to California precisely at that time? Was it only coincidence? Or did they decide *when* I would wake up? Why would they keep me in a coma for so long? Why would they steal a year and a half of my life? What kind of parents are they?

Careful, Jenna.

I was wrong. Lily gets to enjoy her silence.

Agreement

I never asked about the accident. Something told me not to.

Maybe it was the shine of Mother's eyes.

Maybe it was Father's smile that tried too hard.

Maybe it was something deeper inside me that I still can't name.

The Accident.

Like a title. A stop sign. A wall.

It separates me from who I was and who I will be.

I can't ask and they don't offer.

It's a hushed agreement.

Perhaps the only thing

we have ever

agreed upon.

Inside

'We're here.'

Lily's voice is soft. Different. The landscape I wanted to memorize has ribboned away behind me, and I now find myself sitting in a parking lot that I don't remember driving to.

'Jenna.'

That voice again. The soft one of Lily's I barely recognize. How long have we been driving? How long have I been staring out the window and seeing nothing? It sinks in, like sharp teeth in my skin, just how much I still need to know. My fingers grip the seat. I need a word. *Curious. Lost. Angry.* Which one? *Sick?* Is that it? I grasp for a word that isn't there.

'Jenna.'

Scared. The softness of Lily's voice makes it surface. I am scared.

I turn my head to look at her face, wondering at this change in her. 'Why do you hate me?' I ask.

She doesn't answer. She studies my face. Her chest rises, and her head tilts slightly. 'I don't hate you, Jenna,' she finally says. 'I simply don't have room for you.' Harsh words, but her voice is tender and the contradiction is a stony reminder that I am missing something vital. I know the old Jenna Fox would have understood. But the timbre of Lily's voice calms me just the same. I nod, like I understand.

'Come in with me,' she says gently, and she gathers packages from the back seat. I follow her across an empty graveled lot.

A tall whitewashed building, blinding bright against a cold

blue sky, appears to be our destination. My eyes ache from the glare. 'What is this?' I ask.

'The mission. San Luis Rey. I've been in contact with Father Rico for years. We finally get to meet.' We enter through a heavy wooden door in a long white wall. The entrance leads to a shady enclosed cemetery. 'This way,' Lily says, like she has been here before and knows the way. I look at wilted flowers, notes, and stuffed animals that lie on graves and tombstones and feel a brief moment of envy at the remembrances. I see one marker that dates back to 1823, the numbers almost weathered away. Over two hundred years later and still remembered.

I wonder how Lily knows a priest in an ancient mission so far from Boston. We reach the end of the cemetery and come to the great wall of the church which borders it. Lily pulls open yet another large wooden door, and this time we slip into cool blackness and the sweet smell of burning candles, mustiness, and age. My eyes adjust and I see a domed painted ceiling, and then a gilded crucified figure. Christ. *Yes, Christ.* I remember. Lily bends a knee as she crosses in front of the altar and lifts her hand to her forehead, her heart, and then each shoulder with movement that is so swift and natural it is over as soon as it begins. This I don't remember.

I stop and stare at the gilded figure. My eyes travel to the altar and then the baptismal font. There should be a feeling, I think. The room itself demands it, but no feeling is in me. I close my eyes. I'm instantly caught up in a scene playing behind my lids, and I feel cool drops of water on my forehead. Lily's unlined face looms, years younger, and then a man, smiling. He takes my whole body into his hands and kisses my cheek. I see my own hand wave before my face, as small as a butterfly, an infant's hand. I open my eyes. My baptism. I remember it. How is that possible?

Lily waits across the room, poised at another door, expecting me to follow.

'Did my grandfather have black hair?' I ask.

'Yes,' Lily answers. 'You probably saw him in the videos. He didn't die until you were two.'

I never saw him in the videos. 'How did he die?'

'The Aureus epidemic. We had plenty of warnings that something like that could happen and it eventually did. It took him and twenty million people with him.'

'And that was just in this country,' I say.

Lily's eyebrows raise. It is her first glimpse at the facts my brain chooses to hold on to. Her fingers tighten on the iron door handle. 'By then most antibiotics were useless,' she says. 'Somewhere along the line, we took a giant step backward. When I was a child, there were only a handful of vaccines; now there's a vaccine for nearly everything because we've engineered ourselves right into a corner. That's progress?' She looks at me, and a crease deepens between her brows. 'Sometimes we just don't know when we've gone too far.' She opens the door to leave, and a shaft of light cuts across the floor.

'Is that why you gave up being a doctor?'

She stops and turns.

'Because you couldn't save him?' I add. I am only curious, but I see her transform instantly. If she was bitter before, she is stiffness and rage now.

'And *that* would be none of your business,' she answers.

'They have laws now,' I say.

One corner of Lily's mouth turns up. It is not a smile. 'Yes. They do. Entire acts passed by Congress. Scientists can't burp without someone forming a committee to investigate them. Some even go to prison. That in your head, too?'

'No.'

'Didn't think so. I don't think they'd want you to know about that. The problem is, some people think they're above the law. There are plenty of good reasons why we have so much regulation.'

'Like?'

She seems almost amused by the tone of my challenge, surprised, maybe, that I would even question her. I watch her draw up, becoming larger than the Lily I have seen, looking like she is prepared to take me on and a dozen others, too, if necessary.

'Engineering corn to resist pests wiped the original species from the face of the planet. Laws are too late for that,' she says, her eyes drilling into me. 'And a simple thing like overusing antibiotics created a strain of bacteria so deadly it killed my husband and a quarter of the world's population. So that is—'

'Were you?' I see the circular thought she meant to hide from me.

'What?'

'Above the law. When you were a doctor. Did you ever—'

'Yes.' I watch the stiffness of her muscles drain away. 'And I live with that every day of my life.' She turns to leave.

'Lily,' I say to stop her, 'did my grandfather—Did you—Was I baptized?'

'When she was two weeks old,' she says as she walks out the door. 'We were her godparents.' She is gone and never looks back to see if I followed.

•   •   •

Father Rico and Lily sit in the shade of a pepper tree and swap stories. We have already toured the remnants of the ancient mission garden, where the two of them excitedly examined gnarled roots, weeds, and what appeared to be anemic orange trees that were bearing the tiniest of pale fruit. Father Rico proudly proclaimed it the first nursery in California, but the treasure for both of them lies in the seeds and DNA that are left behind.

Their voices rise and some words drift across the expanse of the courtyard.

'Pure.'

'Unadulterated.'

'Original seed.'

'Untouched DNA.'

If I strained I could hear it all, but I don't really need more details than what Father Rico has already given me. He and Lily are both members of the World Seed Preservation Organization, a group committed to preserving original species of plants. Apparently there are few pure species left, due to bioengineering and cross-pollination. The wind, it seems, isn't discriminatory in which kind of plant pollen it blows. Engineered pollen blows just as easily as the original kind and infects all traditional plants in its path. Now I know the deeper meaning to Lily's greenhouse. She and Father Rico seem to see bioengineered plants as a time bomb, much like the Aureus epidemic. Their network of seed enthusiasts are out to save the world. Saviors. Lily saved me once. I wonder how often she thinks about that.

Lily regularly glances my way to make sure I haven't wandered away or started a conversation with anyone. Occasionally someone passes through the courtyard, mostly other priests, but I remain quiet. Lily told me to. 'Your mother would want it that way,' she says.

I see a boy, taller than Father Rico, across the courtyard. He approaches them. His hands are dirty, and he swipes away long cords of black hair spilling in front of his eyes with his forearm. He is...pleasant-looking. I think that's the word. He talks to Father Rico, nods his head, and then glances over at me. I see Lily's face. She has noticed and sits up straighter like she is ready to spring. I think he is going to walk over to me and I look away to discourage him. It works. He says a few more words to Father Rico and goes back the way he came, and I am immediately angry with myself for being so quick to please Lily and Mother. It won't happen again.

Go to Your Room

Mother sips orange juice at the counter, looking over a list of tasks for the day. Lily grates cheese over a bowl of eggs. I sip my nutrients, which are tasteless. I swig down the last of them in a quick gulp and ask, 'Was I a history buff?'

Mother barely looks up from her list. 'A what?'

I decide to rephrase Mr Bender's question. 'Did I like history? Was it my favorite subject?'

Mother smiles and looks back at her list, making a few changes. 'Hardly,' she answers. 'I'm afraid history—and math for that matter—were tutorworthy for you.' She is absorbed again in her planning. Tutorworthy? I must have had an excellent tutor.

I push my empty glass away and announce, 'I'm going to school today.'

Mother drops her pencil and stares at me. Lily stops beating her eggs.

'I assume I didn't graduate during the year I was in a coma, so I still need to finish, right?'

Mother hasn't spoken. Her mouth is open and her head shakes slightly, like my words are ricocheting around inside. Somehow, I find it amusing.

'There are two village charters within walking distance—I checked the directory on the Net—and the Central Academy is just a short drive.'

'You can't drive!' The words shoot out of Mother, and then she says more calmly, 'School is out of the question. You're still recovering—'

'I'm fine—'

Mother stands. '*I said* school is out of the question. Period.'

I hesitate, but then stand, too. 'And I say *it isn't.*'

Mother is shocked into a marble stance. Neither of us speaks. Finally she looks away. She sits back down. She picks up her pencil. She is calm, smooth, practiced, the mother who seems to know where we are going before I do. 'Go to your room, Jenna. You need to rest. Go. Now.'

I am seething. Outraged. Incensed. *The words.* They're finally bubbling up in torrents just when I need them.

But the *will.* It is waning. Mother says I should go to my room. *Go to your room, Jenna. Go to your room.*

I do.

The rage is doubling, multiplying, filling my vision like

a black cloud. I can hardly see as each step brings me closer to my room. *Go to your room, Jenna.* And I am. I am. I collapse on the last stair and rock back and forth silently. What world have I woken up to? What nightmare am I in? Why am I compelled to do as Mother says even when I have a desperate need to do something else? I rock in the dark hollow of the landing, feeling like I am back in the silent vacuum where my voice is never heard. If Jenna Fox was a weak-willed coward, I don't want to be her at all. I hug my arms, trying to squeeze away the world. I hear a sharp voice. It is Mother. She is angry. At me? I did as she asked. I lean near the banister to listen. Lily's voice is angry, too.

'When will you admit you made a mistake?'

'Stop it! You of all people should understand! If it weren't for in vitro, I wouldn't be here. You always called me your miracle. Why can't I have one, too? Why do you get to decide when the miracles will end?'

'It's not natural.'

'Neither was I! You needed help. That's all I wanted—'

I hear a strange noise. A sob?

'Claire.'

'Please,' Mother says. Her voice is soft now. Almost a whisper.

'Claire, you can't keep her hidden from the world. She wants a life. Isn't that what this was all about?'

'It's not that easy. It could be dangerous.'

'Walking across the street can be dangerous, but thousands of people do it every day.'

'I don't mean for her. There are others to consider.'

'Oh. Them.' Lily's voice is mocking. Mother doesn't respond. The conversation seems to be over. I hear dishes clatter and then a chair scraping across the floor. Silence threads through the house like a lace pulling tight, and then I finally hear the scraping of another chair and the sound of Lily sighing herself into place. 'You know I don't care one way or another. I said good-bye eighteen months ago. You can send her back to Boston as far as I'm concerned, but as I see it, you made a decision. Right or wrong, it's done. Now you have to move on. Are you her keeper or her mother?'

I hear a choking sound, and then an almost inaudible 'I don't know'.

Silence follows. No dishes. No chairs. No voices. No bending. Mother is done. So is Lily. Lily, the last person I expected to argue for me. At least I think that's what she did. But she would be just as happy if I were three thousand miles away in Boston. Probably happier. I don't understand. I only know I will not be going to school. Claire said so.

Claire.

I remember now.

I didn't call her Mother. I called her Claire. I am certain of it. I finish the ascent of the stairs. I go to my room. Claire told me to. I think I hate her.

Jenna Fox / Year Ten

I know the meaning, but I check again to be sure.

> **Hate** v. *1. Intense dislike, extreme aversion or hostility.*
> *2. To dislike passionately. 3. To detest.*

There is a better word for Mother. *Aggravating*, maybe.

But I think Lily is wrong. She does hate me. Her aversion is extreme. She nearly shakes me with her constant sideways glances. She hasn't spoken more than four words to me in as many days, but since she's been out in the greenhouse from dawn until dusk, it has been easy to avoid me. Our worlds only intersect briefly in the morning when the three of us sit at the kitchen table and in the evening when we return there. I have been in my room watching discs. Mother asked me to. Her desperation for me to be who I was has intensified. As the Cotswold sees improvement, workers coming and going and restoring, it is like she expects to see the same measure of improvement in me. Restored shingles. Restored flooring. Restored Jenna.

I don't want restoration. I want a life. Now. I want to move on. Those were Lily's words. It is ironic that her words should become my own.

But I watch the discs.

Because Mother told me to.

I am halfway through Year Ten of Jenna Fox. I see a pretty girl. Her blond silky hair wags in a ponytail across her back. I have already seen her at diving lessons, another ballet recital, practicing piano, and now I see her running across a field kicking a soccer ball. She is impossibly busy. Her life is so full I can hardly take it in, the complete opposite of the empty-life Jenna I am now.

She kicks the ball to a teammate, who in turn kicks the ball into the goal. A horn sounds. Fists fly into the air along with shouts. Teammates hug and lift one another, and Jenna is in the midst of it all. I hear Father and Mother, unseen behind the camera, cheering and finally calling me over. I run to them. I acknowledge their

47

congratulations. I smile. I toss my head back to call to a friend, and I notice something for the first time. A thin red line just under my chin.

'Pause,' I blurt out. 'Back. Pause.' The disc player follows my commands. I look closer at the still picture. 'Zoom.' The thin red line becomes what I suspected. A scar.

I walk to my bathroom mirror and tilt my face back. I run my fingertips up the length of my throat. I feel. I search.

There is no scar.

It's been seven years since that video was filmed. Do scars disappear in seven years?

A Glimpse

It's been twenty-five days since I woke up.

Eight days since I went to the mission.

Six days since the new front walkway was laid.

Five days since the plumbing fixtures were replaced.

Three days since I last saw Mr Bender through my window.

Three days of rain and 4,287 cold beads of water beating against my windowpanes.

I'm good at math after all.

Without friends and a packed schedule to keep me busy, keeping track of time and numbers has become a prime source of entertainment. Watching the collecting rivulets of rain on my window has become a close second.

February in California is cold. Not as cold as Boston. Not nearly. The Net Report says it has dropped to a low of fifty-four degrees. 'Oh, my,' Lily had mocked. The temperature varies very little. Boredom reigns on all levels. The rain is a welcome change. I have seen the pond swell and the creek surge. I press my palm against the glass, imagining the drops on my skin, imagining where they started out, where they will go, feeling them like a river, rushing, combining, becoming something greater than how they started out.

I spend time on the Net. Mr Bender said there isn't a thing you can't learn about your neighbors there. Since he is the only neighbor I know, I learn things about him. He is famous. A recluse. There are no pictures of him. Few people have ever met him. Quirky artist. And more.

I type in the name Jenna Fox. I am overwhelmed with the hits. *There are thousands.* Which one am I? I turn off the Net and realize I don't even know my middle name. It's too much work, trying to become who I am, always having to ask others what I should already know. I lie on my bed staring at the ceiling. For hours maybe.

Other thoughts replay, collect, finger out into more thoughts.

Mr Bender's birds and my untouchable palms...

...a watery blood-bead on my knee...

...a baptism I remember...

...and visitors.

I had visitors last night. Kara and Locke came to me again. In my deepest sleep, they shook me. *Jenna, Jenna.* I opened my eyes, but their voices stayed in my ears. I hear their voices even now. *Hurry, Jenna. Come. Hurry.*

Hurry where?

I see us at the Commons, the memory so vivid I can still smell the freshly mowed grass. We sit at the base of the George Washington Monument, squeezing close for shade, our legs stretched out before us in the long afternoon shadow. We are ditching our Sociology Seminar, and Kara is filling every space with nervous chatter, and when she laughs her black bobbed hair shakes like a skirt at her shoulders. Locke keeps suggesting that we should go. 'No!' Kara and I say together. It's too late. Too late. And then the three of us are laughing again, exhilarated, bolstered together in our defiance.

We are not comfortable with it. We are rule-followers. This is new to us, and our courage comes from each other. I lean over and kiss Locke. Hard on the lips. We explode in more laughter, and snot spurts from our noses. Kara repeats the kiss, and we are limp with our howling. I ache with the remembering.

I roll from my bed to the floor and lean back against the wall, the way I leaned back that day in Boston. I had friends. Good friends.

A Curve

Mother is at the Netbook when I enter the kitchen. She is talking to Father. I have talked to her little more than I have to Lily in the past few days. She is busy and distant. Lily is in the pantry rattling boxes.

'Morning,' Mother says and returns to her conversation with Father.

'Jenna?' Father calls.

'Morning, Father,' I say.

'Come here, Angel.'

I stand behind Mother and look over her shoulder so he can see me.

'You're looking good,' he says. 'How are you feeling?'

'Fine.'

'Any lapses? Pain? Anything unusual?'

'No.'

'Good. Good.' He repeats himself a third time, and I sense he is filling time.

'Something wrong?' I ask.

'No. Not at all. I think your mother wants to have a talk with you, though, so I'll be going. Talk to you tomorrow.' He clicks off.

A talk. She frightens me with her control and sureness. I don't want to talk, but I am sure we will. Claire commands and it happens.

'Sit down,' she says.

I do.

Lily walks out of the pantry and leans against the counter, her own busyness suddenly gone out of her. Mother looks like she is going to regurgitate last night's dinner.

'You're starting school tomorrow,' she says. 'It's only at the local charter. It's the closest one, so you can walk for the days that they meet. Their emphasis is ecosystem studies, but there is nothing I can do about that. It will just have to do. The others are too far, too crowded, and too—well, they simply need too many forms that we can't provide right now. You're all registered, and they're expecting you. Unless you've changed your mind about going to school.'

After a long pause I realize her last sentence is a question. 'No,' I answer. 'I haven't changed my mind.' I am still backtracking, trying to absorb everything she has thrown at me. School? Tomorrow? I thought it was out of the question. How did this happen? I pause in sorting out the turnaround, and I finally notice her.

Her eyes are glassy puddles. Her hands rest in her lap, weakly turned upward. The steady stream of words has ended, and she looks spent from the effort.

'Are you happy?' she asks.

I nod. Is it a trick? This is not what she wants. What is she *really* trying to do? 'Yes. Thank you,' I say. She pulls me close, and I feel her uneven breaths against my neck. Her grip is tight and I think she won't let go, but then she pushes back my shoulders and she smiles. The limp hands tighten, the eyes blink, and with a deep breath she summons the infinite control that is Claire's.

'I'm meeting with carpenters this morning, but I will talk to you more about it this afternoon.' She hesitates for a long moment, then adds, 'The rain's stopped. Why don't you go out for a walk while you can?' Her face is pale.

A walk, too?

I can't respond. All I can think of is the gilded figure hanging on the wall in Lily's church. Mother's lifeblood is flowing out of her.

'Thank you,' I say again and head for the door, but before I leave the room, I see Lily close her eyes at the kitchen sink and her hand brushes her forehead, her heart, and finally each shoulder.

Plea

I hear sobbing.

And then a Hail Mary.

I hear a mumbling of prayers. And bargaining, too.

Jesus. Jesus.

Jesus.

Pleading and moaning.

In the darkest place that revisits me over and over again.

And for the first time I recognize the voice.

It is Lily.

A Walk

I am out the door in seconds. I am going to school. Tomorrow.
I hurry down the walkway. Will Mother change her mind? I
glance over my shoulder to make sure she is not following me.
Freedom. It feels as crisp and breezy as the open sky. But then I
remember her pale face. Her tentative decision. My pace quickens.
Distance is my savior. I flee from my closed world into one I
haven't met yet.

Them.

Mother said it could be dangerous. *For them.* Is she afraid I will
hurt others? My classmates? I wouldn't. But maybe the old Jenna
would? Did I hurt Kara and Locke? Is that why they aren't my
friends anymore?

There is Mr Bender. He counts as a friend. I will visit him.

With the swelling of the creek, I can't pass between our yards,
so I follow the streets around to his house. I don't know his
address or what his house looks like from the front, but I know,
like ours, it is the last house on his street.

Even though the rain has stopped, the gutters are still like small
rivers. Leaving our sidewalk to walk in the street, I must leap to
get over the expanse. I walk down the middle of the road. The air
smells of wet soil and eucalyptus. This time tomorrow I will be in
school. I will be making more friends. I will be owning a life. The
life of Jenna Fox. It will be mine, whatever *it* may be.

Our neighbor's house, the massive Tudor, is dark and quiet.
Same with the next house. But at the sprawling Craftsman I see
activity. A small white dog barks at me through the bars of a gate.

I stop and watch him. A woman calls to me, and I turn my head toward the front drive, where she sweeps the litter of the storm.

'Sorry,' she says. 'He thinks he's a guard dog. Don't worry, though. He's all bark. Wouldn't hurt a flea.'

I nod. I never thought he would hurt me. He's a dog. He barks. Should I have been afraid? Is this what all neighbors do? Warn you about things? The way Mr Bender warned me about the white house at the end of my street? Is it a nicety that means nothing, but one of the many other subtleties that has become muddled inside of me? Am I missing something, or are they?

The woman lifts her hand, holds it there, and then waves. A smile follows. 'You okay?' she asks.

'Are you?' I ask. Maybe I need to be concerned about my neighbors, too? She returns abruptly to her sweeping and I leave.

Even though it is morning, the sky is still dark with clouds and there are lights on in the next house. The white house. As I get closer, I can see a glowing chandelier through a large window over the door. More lights shine behind other curtained windows. The pillars on either side of the door are cracked, lines running the length of them, bits of concrete missing. I imagine they are bits that fell away with the last earthquake and were never repaired, but still, the house looks to be well cared for. Better than ours. It is not a frightening house, at least not what lies outside. The front door opens, catching me. I try to resume my walk before I am noticed, but it is too late. A shadowed figure reaches for a paper on the porch but then stops and straightens without retrieving it. He steps out. It is a boy. Like the boy I saw at the mission, he is tall and pleasant-looking, but his hair is as white as the other boy's hair was black. It is short and uncombed, a scuffle of waves pointing in different directions.

'Hello,' he calls. His voice is pleasant, too.

'Hello.'

'You new in the neighborhood?'

'Yes.'

'Welcome. I'm Dane.' He smiles. Even from the street I can see the whiteness of his teeth.

'Hello,' I say again.

I want to leave, but my feet seem stapled to the ground. He is bare-chested and his pajama-bottoms hang dangerously low. He pulls them up and shrugs. Was I staring?

'I better go,' he says. 'Nice meeting you.'

'Bye, Dane,' I answer, and miraculously my feet are released and I continue on my walk.

When your life has had few events to occupy it, it's amazing how a simple encounter can seem like an entire three-act play. I replay it over and over in my head while I continue on my way to Mr Bender's house. Dane. White house. White pajamas. White teeth. There was nothing frightening about it, except the way I was frozen on the street.

Persona

Finding his house is easy. Left. Left. Left. A ten-minute walk at most. He is surprised to see me but invites me in.

'Coffee?'

'I can't drink. I mean I don't drink coffee,' I say.

Mr Bender stirs cream into his. He offers me juice, milk, bagels, and muffins. I say no to them all. 'I'm on a special diet,' I tell him.

'Allergies?'

'No. Just special.'

He nods. It is a nod that says, yes, I know. *What does he know?* He says there isn't a thing you can't find out about your neighbors on the Net. Has he found out something about me?

'Did you get your pictures of the pine serpent?' I ask.

'Yes. Dozens. I'm trying to choose the best ones to send to my agent.'

'Did you get some pictures with the birds?'

'A few. But the few were fairly amazing. I got lucky.'

'May I see them?'

'The pictures?'

'No. The birds.'

Our footsteps make whooshing sounds on the rain-soaked ground. Puddles spot the pathway into the garden. With his long stride, Mr Bender steps over them, but I step in them. 'I don't know how many there'll be,' he says, 'with the storm and all.'

All I want is one.

We sit on the log bench. He's right. There are not many. Only two, the rest still huddled away from the storm. But the two that come will land only on his hand.

After twenty minutes, he puts the birdseed away and we walk back to the house. He pours himself another cup of coffee and I shuffle through photos of the pine serpent.

'Don't worry about it, Jenna.'

What makes him think I'm worried? And why should it matter so much whether a small brown bird lands on my hand anyway? What makes him think I care?

'Some things take time,' he says.

Too many things take time. I've lost so much time already. A year and a half might as well be a lifetime for me. 'I don't have time to spare,' I tell him.

He laughs. 'Sure you do. You're only seventeen. You have lots of time.'

I set the pictures in my hand down on the table.

I never told him I was seventeen.

'Where did you find that out, Mr Bender?' I ask. 'On the Net? Am I one of the neighbors who you find things out about?'

He refills his coffee mug. 'Yes.' He's not apologetic.

'You're not embarrassed about your snooping?'

'It's not snooping. I need to know about my neighbors.'

Maybe so. Maybe I do, too. 'Then I have a confession to make,' I tell him. 'You're not the only snoop. I did some checking, and I found out a few things about you, too.'

'Oh?' His brows arch, and he sits down opposite me.

'Have you had surgery, Mr Bender? Or maybe you simply have excellent genes?'

'Meaning?'

'You look like you're about forty-five. Fifty at most.'

He doesn't reply.

'But Clayton Bender the artist was born eighty-four years ago. You either hold your age really well, or…?'

'You expect me to fill that one in?'

'No. I've already figured out you can't be him. No one's genes are that good. I just don't know who you really are. A serial killer, maybe?'

He smiles. 'You've got quite an imagination. Nothing that dramatic, I'm afraid.' He takes a long sip from his mug. 'But still serious enough it needs to remain a secret. Only a few people know. My agent, for one. He helps build the quirky-artist persona to keep people away. You're right. I'm not Clayton Bender, but I took his name almost thirty years ago.'

'Your own name wasn't good enough?'

'The name, yes. But the life that went with it, no.'

'Where's the real Mr Bender?'

'He passed away.'

'Did you kill him?'

He laughs. 'No, Jenna, I promise you his passing was quite natural.'

'How did you meet him?'

He stands and walks over to the kitchen sink, pouring the rest of his coffee out. 'I ran away when I was sixteen. I had no other options.' He turns back to face me. 'I got mixed up with some people who could do me some serious harm. A friend gave me some money and his car, and I ended up on the other side of the country on Bender's doorstep. He was a loner out in the desert and needed a worker, so I helped him out and he helped me, no questions asked. I stayed with him for three years.'

'He was an artist then?'

'Of sorts.' He smiles and shrugs, joining me at the table again. 'He got by with a small Net business—grinding and then selling natural pigments to artists all over the world—and the rest of the time he wandered the desert collecting stones. He piled them into little monuments wherever he took a notion. I didn't understand it, but I helped him. In a strange way, it helped me not to think. Maybe that's why he did it, too. Then one day he went out ahead of me looking for stones, and when I caught up with him, he was dead. I never found out what it was. Heart attack or stroke. I don't know. I buried him and gave him his own monument and then I waited for another year, thinking someone would show up. Family, friends, someone to claim the house, but no one ever came. In the meantime, I just kept stacking the stones. I lived off the money he had stashed away, but I knew that couldn't last forever, and then one day it finally occurred to me. I didn't have to hide out forever. I could be Clayton Bender. I had his birth certificate and other documents, and not a soul in the world seemed to know him. I've been him ever since.'

'And your old life? Do you ever miss it?'

'Parts. Mostly I regret that I never saw my parents again.'

'Or your best friend?'

He shrugs and looks away so I can't see his eyes. 'Now you know my secret,' he says. 'Will you keep it?'

'I have no one to tell. And I wouldn't even if I did.'

'Good. You ready to tell me your secrets?'

'I don't have any,' I say. 'None that I remember, at least.'

It occurs to me that Mr Bender is much more clever at finding information about Jenna Fox on the Net than I am. If he knows I am seventeen, what else does he know? Secrets that I don't even know? My hands tremble. I have never seen them tremble before. I stare at them.

'Jenna?'

I clasp my hands together to make them still. For the first time,

I notice they don't interlace smoothly. It feels like I have twelve fingers instead of ten. I keep reworking them, reclasping, but it still feels awkward. Why won't they lace together?

'Jenna? You all right?'

My hands.

I shove them both beneath my thighs, out of sight. *He made it his business to know.* I look at him. 'What else did you find out about me, Mr Bender?'

'I don't think I—'

'Please.'

'I read that you were injured in an accident. They didn't expect you to survive.'

The room spins, and I hold on to the table. Worse, I feel like I am on the edge of shutting down. It's as though, spoken aloud, the word *accident* is a switch, and it's making everything inside me go black. Is that why I avoid it with Mother and Father? I struggle to focus. *Find your way. Make it your business.* 'What kind?'

'Of accident?'

'Yes. That.'

'A car accident.'

A *car* accident? Why did I think it was something else? Something more terrible? There are thousands of car accidents every day. It is practically common. *A car accident.* I can almost say it out loud. Except I wasn't expected to survive—and I did. That is not common.

'Anything else?'

'The article was more about your dad. Anything he does is news, and he was taking a leave of absence from his work because of your condition. Since you were underage, a lot of information

61

was unavailable, but the *Boston Globe* managed to find out that the nurses thought your condition was pretty grave.' He pauses. Is he retrieving information or planning a lie? I watch his eyes carefully. His pupils dart to the left and then back to me. 'That was about all the article said, Jenna.'

A lie.

Does he know I have no memory? *What else?* But curiously, he still seems to want to be my friend, so I drop it. For now. 'Did I pass?' I ask.

'Pass?'

'The Bender Neighbor Investigation?'

He smiles. 'You passed the day I met you, Jenna. You gave me honesty and attitude. I liked that.'

'I don't remember giving you anything.'

'*Attitude,* Jenna. You walked right up to me. Told me what you thought of my work. You weren't afraid of anything.'

But I'm afraid of everything. Myself. Mother. Lily. Friends who haunt me in the night. Even going to school, which is something I asked for. If I have attitude, it is hiding somewhere deep, someplace I'm afraid I may never find.

Jenna Fox / Year Twelve

Jenna is at the shore. A pitchfork is in her hands. Cords of hair whip from her ponytail across her face. She smiles at the camera and says, 'Come on, Mom, put it down and help me!' At twelve years old, I still called her Mom. When did I begin calling her Claire? I can't recall, but I feel the hardness of the word on my lips.

The camera wobbles, and Claire's voice is loud. 'In a minute. Let me get a little more first.'

Was this a family getaway? A day at the beach? Every aspect of Jenna's life is recorded. Father comes into view with a silver pail in hand, and he waves it in front of my face. 'All *mine,*' he teases. 'I won't go hungry! Can't say the same for you two.'

Jenna laughs, this person that is me, and calls, 'He has a hundred quahogs, Mom! Put that down, or we'll starve!' Jenna thrusts her pitchfork into the sand and the camera zooms in on her sandy feet, then glides up the length of her body, like every inch is being adored. It finally stops on my face. It rests there. Caressing. Watching. Watching what? The enthusiasm? The ruddy cheeks? The anticipation? Watching all the breaths, heart-beats, and hopes of Matthew and Claire Fox? For a moment, I can see the weight of it in Jenna's face. My face. 'Mom!' Jenna pleads. The camera wobbles, is turned off, and a new scene appears, focusing on a campfire—

'Stop!' The disc obeys. *A blanket. A blue one. A canteen.*

I think I know what comes next.

A flutter runs through me. *I know.* I picture a scene, fully formed. Jenna, cross-legged on a blue plaid blanket on the sand. A mug of steaming hot chocolate in my hands. Hot chocolate with three fat marshmallows. I *loved* hot chocolate. Taste! I am shocked at my first memory of taste. How could I forget taste? Chunk after chunk pieces together. It is like a window has been opened and memories are breezing through it. Days. Weeks. Three weeks of details collect and run through my mind, every one remembered and sharp.

I pull myself closer to the screen on my desk. My head vibrates.

'Play,' I command. The scene shifts from the campfire to me. I'm sitting on a blue blanket. I lift a mug of hot chocolate to my lips and offer a frothy, chocolate-mustached grin.

'Stop.' I lay my head on my desk. I close my eyes and soak in what it means.

I knew. A whole chunk of my life is mine again.

Three whole weeks' worth. It seems like a lifetime.

My eyes blink open. 'Mother!' I call. I race from my room and down the stairs to the kitchen. 'Lily!'

No one answers. I see Mother out the window, talking with a workman and pointing to panes in the greenhouse. Lily is no doubt somewhere within. I run to the pantry and search for ingredients. I pull cocoa and then sugar from the shelves. *Marshmallows! Lily has marshmallows, too!* I tuck the bag beneath my arm and let them all tumble onto the kitchen counter. Milk! A sauce pot! I remember! I pour. I stir. I make sense of a stove I have never used before. I feel full, powerful, like I haven't felt since I woke up. *I'm making hot chocolate. I love hot chocolate!* I search the cupboards for a mug. I pull the largest one I can find from the shelf and pour the steaming mixture in. I rip open the bag of marshmallows, and just as I plop them in, Lily and Mother come in through the back door. They stop and stare at me and the helter-skelter mess I have made.

'I remember! I love hot chocolate!'

I raise the mug like a toast to celebrate this new memory. I expect a smile—at least from Mother—but instead, as I bring the mug to my lips, her face wrinkles in horror and she yells, 'No!'

Taste

Maybe I don't like hot chocolate.

And maybe the three weeks' worth of memories aren't real at all.

Maybe I don't remember sneaking on makeup in the bathroom
    at school.

Or completing a double pirouette and finishing as gracefully
    as if I really did have wings.

Or snuggling on the sofa with a golden dog I named Hunter.

The hot chocolate was tasteless.

Just like my nutrients.

I know you can forget a lot of things,

but how can you forget taste?

When the mug slipped from my fingers,

Lily caught it.

And hardly any spilled on the floor.

School

I'm certain it is Claire's fault. Everything. Why does she whimper and cower so? Is she guilty? She cried when I dropped the mug. I wanted to hit her. *It's mine, dammit. Mine.* But it must be hers, too, with the way she takes it on. It is like she owns every shortcoming I have. Maybe she just plain owns me. She tried to explain it away. *It's temporary. Your taste will return. You shouldn't have food anyway.* I spent the next hour locked in my bathroom, staring at my tongue. It's normal. Rough and pink and fleshy. What's wrong is somewhere else inside. Something that is disconnected within me. I don't trust her. She hovers, smiles, cries, and controls. Too much of everything. I need to get away from her.

I open the car door. She opens hers, too.

'No,' I say. 'I'm seventeen. I can do this on my own.'

'But, Jenna—'

I've learned how to smile in the space of just a few short weeks. I'm learning how to control, too. 'Claire,' I say, to hold her to the seat.

She shuts her door. 'That again?' she says, looking straight ahead. She is hurt. Everything backs up inside me. School, control, distrust, and doubt, they all get shoved behind the hurt on her face.

I hear words, words from long ago that were snarled inside me. *I'm sorry. So sorry.* Words that were trapped in my head and couldn't be said, frozen behind lips that wouldn't move. And that made me want to say them more.

It's okay, darling. It's all right. Shhh. Everything will be fine. Claire answering over and over again when I hadn't even spoken, looking into my eyes and reflecting all the pain she saw.

I get out of the car and lean down, looking at her through the window. Claire forces a smile. Her eyes cling to me. *I'm so sorry.* She rolls down the window. I say a dozen more redundant things— things we have already discussed—just to keep her from talking. I will take my afternoon nutrients. I will not discuss the accident. I will be outside at three o'clock. I will call if I need her.

I'm afraid she will have a last-minute change of heart, will control me in that way she does and force me back into the car just by saying my name. It is like we are both fighting for control of Jenna Fox.

'I'll be fine,' I finally say, and thankfully, like a miracle, she leaves without saying another word.

I turn and face the village charter. School. It is nothing more than an abandoned real estate office. I see the defunct sign dismantled and leaning against the side, almost obscured by overgrown weeds. Dusty blinds hang in the windows. A pale coat of yellow paint makes a faint attempt at sprucing it up. It looks more like an old farmhouse. Maybe it once was. Their emphasis is ecosystems? I went to a central academy in Boston—Claire told me—but even before she confirmed it, I knew. I remember when Kara, Locke, and I ditched a seminar. We were afraid but hoped we wouldn't be missed among the hundreds of students who were in our class. I don't know what a charter is like except that it is small. Hundreds, maybe thousands of students smaller than an academy. They go to school only a few days a week. What kind of students choose to go to such a small, run-down school when they could attend an academy with everyone else? It is different in every way, but since I can't remember too much about the old ways, it shouldn't matter to me. *Why did I want to go to school again?*

I walk up the steps and go inside.

Dane

'You must be Jenna.'

The room is small. I could almost spread my arms out and touch each wall. It holds a desk and a large round woman, who is smiling at me. She already knows my name. I stare at her shocking orange hair.

I want to leave and flag down Claire.

'It is Jenna, right?'

'Yes,' I say. 'Who are you?'

'Mitch.' She remains seated but holds out her hand. I take it. It is puffy and hot and amazingly strong as she squeezes my fingers tight. 'I'm the facilitator, which means I do about everything around here.'

'Except pull weeds?'

She hesitates for a moment and then laughs. 'You're going to fit right in around here, Jenna.' She reaches behind her and hands me a small Netbook. 'I just need you to fill out a questionnaire and then I'll take you back with the others.'

I am relieved that the questions are basic, mostly wanting to know my interests and what I see as my strengths and weaknesses. Strengths? Easy. I don't hold grudges. It's difficult to hold a grudge when you can't remember what they are. Weaknesses?

Would *forgetful* be understating it? I go for something easier to interpret. Strength: history buff. Weakness: none. The last question makes me pause: why did you choose a school with an ecosystem emphasis?

I didn't. Claire did.

'Finished?' Mitch asks.

Close enough. 'Yes.' I close the Netbook and hand it back to her. I remember why I wanted to come to school. I need friends. Not questions. I have enough of those already.

'Fine then, let's go meet the other students—and Dr Rae. She's your principal teacher. Director, really. Most of the curriculum is self-guided, and each of you takes on the role of collaborator-teacher. But she will tell you all about that.' She slides the Netbook into a file with four others, stands, and guides me through a doorway and down a hall that creaks under her heavy footsteps.

She opens the last door, and I follow her in. It is a large room with modern furnishings. At one end are chairs and three long library desks. At the other end of the room are a half dozen Net stations. In the center, taking up most of the room, are two worn leather couches and four sling chairs. I note that the chairs' fabric matches Mitch's cheddar-cheese hair. Two boys and one girl occupy them. None of them look like they could be a Dr Rae.

'Where's Rae?' Mitch asks.

'She's conferencing,' the girl offers.

Mitch raises her eyebrows. 'With Mr Collins, I presume?'

No one answers. I conclude it wasn't a question, because Mitch appears satisfied and moves on. 'Let me introduce Jenna.

She's going to be joining your group.'

The boy whose back is to me stands up, turns, and I recognize him. He is the boy from the mission with the dirty hands and black hair. 'Ethan,' he says. He doesn't offer a smile or a hand, but his eyes are clearly focused on mine.

The girl struggles to get up. She has a brace in each hand. 'I hope to lose these soon,' she says. She tucks one brace under her arm and reaches out her other hand. 'I'm Allys.' Her hand is stiff and cool.

Mitch turns, not waiting for the rest of the introductions. 'Rae will be in soon, I'm sure. Carry on,' she says as she leaves.

The other boy steps forward, wipes his palms on his jeans, and then stuffs them in his pockets, apparently deciding not to offer one after all. He is thin and small. 'I'm Gabriel. Hi.'

'Hello,' I say to them all. 'Where's the rest of your class?'

'This is it, cupcake. Welcome to Freaks Unlimited.'

I spin around. A young man fills the doorway.

'Shut up, Dane.'

Dane ignores Ethan and smiles at me. 'So this is our latest addition. *Very* nice. Ethan's right for once—nothing freakish about you.' He carefully looks me over, like he is trying to decide something. 'We've met?'

'A couple of days ago. I was outside—'

'My house. Yes. I remember. So *you're* Jenna Fox.'

I never told him my last name. *Did Mitch?*

Dane saunters past me and plops onto the couch. He is full of smiles. He seems to be the happiest of the group.

'You can put your stuff in there, if you like,' Allys tells me, pointing to a cabinet behind the library tables. All I have is a small knapsack containing my vial of nutrients, but I go ahead and walk to the other end of the room to put it away.

'Wrong!' Dane calls out. 'I stand corrected. You *are* one of us.'

I turn back to him. 'Pardon me?' I say.

'Your feet?'

'Leave it, Dane.'

'What? We're supposed to pretend she doesn't walk funny? Right, Allys. And you've got all your digits, and Ethan has a magnetic personality.'

'Eat it,' Ethan says and falls back into one of the sling chairs.

Gabriel slinks into the corner and sits at a Net station, looking small and thankful to be under the radar.

Allys works her way back to her chair. 'Learn to ignore him, Jenna. The rest of us do.'

I walk funny?

'It's okay,' I say. 'I had an—' *Don't discuss the accident.* '—an illness. I'll be better soon.'

'That's what we all say,' Dane answers.

Dr Rae breezes into the room. 'Jenna, you're here. Welcome! And you've all been getting acquainted. That's nice.'

Nice.

I need to look that word up again.

Ethan

I get a turn at 'conferencing' with Rae. She doesn't like to be called doctor. She says we are all 'learning colleagues'. She tells me details of her life. Since we are colleagues, she says, I should know as much about her as she knows about me. She is forty-eight, older than Claire, but she looks about ten years younger. I wonder what has aged Claire so. She says she moved here from Ohio when she was a teenager. It was hard for her to move at that age.

'Was your move from New York difficult for you?' she asks.

New York. *Right.* Mother says not to tell we are from Boston. Reporters are always bothering Father, and she wants peace and quiet.

'No,' I say. 'I slept right through it.'

She smiles. 'It sounds like you're flexible, Jenna—and have a sense of humor. That will take you far.'

I let her think what she wants.

She tells me that the three days a week we meet, teacher-collaborators will instruct on core subjects. State requirements are modified as much as possible to complement the ecosystems emphasis. This morning while she and I conference, Ethan is leading a discussion with the others on *Walden.* Apparently, literature is Ethan's strength. Gabriel is teacher-collaborator for problem-solving and logic. Allys leads science and ethics. Dane leads art explorations. Rae fills in the holes.

'Would you be interested in leading us in historical explorations? We're just about to begin a discussion of Easter Island and the—'

'Easter Island was settled approximately A.D. 300 by the Rapa Nui.

By A.D.1000 deforestation was under way to satisfy the islanders' demand for moai construction. The loss of forest resulted in erosion, which in turn accelerated the rapid decline of trees on the island. By 1600, the failing resources of the island could no longer support the population, and as a result, cannibalism—'

I notice Rae's peculiar expression, so I stop.

'Uh, yes, I guess you do know your history,' she says.

'I'm familiar with *Walden,* too, if Ethan needs help.' I'm more than familiar—I could recite it word for word, but I don't tell her that. I'm startled at this revelation myself. Until she mentioned it, I had no recollection of *Walden.* I must have loved literature, too.

'I see.' She looks back at my questionnaire. I know what she is going to say before the words leave her mouth. *Weaknesses? You have no weaknesses?* It skips through me. Catches. *Weakness. Please, Jenna. We need you.* Why do I see Kara's and Locke's faces? They couldn't have been my weaknesses. They feel more like my strengths.

'And no weaknesses?'

'I didn't write them down.'

'Would you like to share?'

Share?

I'm afraid.

I'm lost.

I have no friends. It keeps coming back to that. Why does it bother me so?

I have no friends.

Which weakness shall I tell her?

'I walk funny,' I say, and she is satisfied with that.

•   •   •

Morning collaborations continue until eleven. I correct Ethan twice in his evaluations of *Walden.* I want to be his friend. Friends help friends.

It is my second time that prompts him to raise his voice. 'But it was his rejection of materialism and the Industrial Revolution that was the point of his move to Walden Pond and the strength of the entire—'

'Not true,' I tell him. 'It was a private journey as much as a public one. He was searching for his personal essence as much as he was making a political statement.'

'But—'

'In his final conclusion he says, *It is life near the bone where it is sweetest.* And building on that he says, *I sat at a table where were rich food and wine in abundance, and obsequious attendance, but sincerity and truth were not; and I went away hungry from the inhospitable board.*'

'But what about—'

'And of course, much earlier he plainly states, *I went to the woods because I wished to live deliberately . . . to live deep and suck out all the marrow of life . . . to—*'

'I get it,' Ethan snaps.

Dane, Allys, and Gabriel stare at me. Ethan looks away. Rae is quickly flipping through *Walden,* running her fingers down the pages. Finally she raises her eyes to me, too.

Dane stands. 'The only thing Thoreau and I have in common is that we're both hungry,' he says. 'I'm outta here.'

Rae looks at her watch. 'Eleven. Yes, it's time for our break. Thank you, Jenna. And you, too, Ethan.'

Dane is already out the door. Rae is drawn away by Mitch and something more important than me.

The others stand awkwardly. I can see I've upset the balance. Do they have to include the new girl who walks funny in their break plans? Do they have to redefine boundaries? Do they have to make room for someone who interrupted Ethan when she should have kept her big mouth shut? Why can I see that now, when it's too late?

'Break is for two hours,' Allys says. 'Time to eat, work on personal projects, conference—Rae's big on that. You can do whatever you want.'

Gabriel gestures over his shoulder. 'We usually go across the street and get something to eat at the market. Everyone's kind of on their own.'

On their own. Right. I get it.

I nod. 'Then I'll just stay—'

'Want to come?' Ethan asks.

Allys

Allys removes her leg and props it against the table. 'I'm not supposed to take them off at school, but this one still bothers me.' She massages her stump. Gabriel and Ethan go on eating their lunches. I stare at the stump and then the artificial leg. 'Does this bother you?' she asks. 'I can put it back—'

'No. I'm just surprised. I didn't realize. Were you injured somehow?'

'No. I had a bacterial infection. Worse than most. Antibiotics weren't touching it, and by the time they were able to get a Restricted Antibiotic Waiver, I had already lost one leg. This one, actually.' She runs her fingers over her stump and grimaces. 'I guess the first is hardest to lose.'

'Your other leg is artificial, too?'

'And my arms. I also had some organ damage, which is why I have to take this mountain of medicine.' She swallows a handful of pills and downs them with water.

My eyes shift from her stump to her hands. 'They look so—'

'Real?'

I nod.

'I hear that a lot. Amazing what they can do these days.' She pulls up her sleeve, and I can see a barely perceptible line where artificial meets real skin. 'They even customized it with my original moles and freckles.'

'Yeah,' Gabriel adds through a mouthful of food, 'she has a whole constellation on her other arm.' Ethan doesn't say anything. He just watches me while he eats.

'Sure, nice cosmetics, but I still have phantom pains. It's only been six months, so I am hoping that will go away, too. The biofeedback treatments worked on the others, but not on this one for some reason.' She stops rubbing her stump and picks up her sandwich. I watch her artificial fingers delicately bend and adjust around the bread, just like they are real. I am aware of prosthetic devices, but I think this is the first time I have seen them so close. The skin looks as real as my own. Allys glances at me, and I look away. I already have one strike against me by showing up Ethan. I don't want another by ogling her. They've invited me into their circle. I want to stay here.

I sit back in my chair, trying to look relaxed. A small dining area is carved out of one corner of the market. It holds two small tables, each with four chairs. They're crowded next to the juice aisle. Gabriel and Allys both got ready-made sandwiches from the refrigerated section. Ethan bought an apple, a bean-and-cheese burrito, and a bottle of milk. Even though he invited me to come, he seems reluctant to talk to me. I'm trying to keep my mouth shut, but since I'm not eating, it isn't easy.

'What about Dane?' I ask. 'I thought he was hungry.'

Gabriel smirks. 'Dane doesn't eat with us.'

'Because we're freaks?' I ask.

'Speak for yourself!' Ethan snaps. His voice is loud and pocks the air between us.

I don't know what to say. I didn't mean that I thought he was a freak. I was just repeating Dane's words, but I'm afraid to even explain that. I might appear like I'm correcting him again. I look out the window, a jammed-up feeling growing inside. Am I going to cry? Or is it something else? My eyes are dry, but I feel like something wants to burst out of me. I focus on the empty road outside. Hold back. Hold it in. *Keep your mouth shut, Jenna. Keep it shut. Shut. Shut.*

'Well, Dane was certainly right about one thing,' I say, turning from the window to look straight into Ethan's eyes.

'What's that?' he asks, daring me to answer.

'You do have a magnetic personality.'

Wonderful timing, Jenna. Now is not the time for my attitude to come out of hiding.

Gabriel stops chewing, and his eyes grow wide. Allys sets her sandwich aside. Ethan sits, stunned, like I just slapped him across the face. The tension holds us like a shock of electricity, and then something odd happens. Allys chuckles. A little snort at first. And then a deep expelling of air that comes all the way up from her belly. Her laughter snags Gabriel, and puffs of air fill his cheeks, and then in the next breath, Ethan and I are snorting, too, unable to maintain our scowls. Pieces of bread fly from Gabriel's mouth, and we all howl louder, until finally Allys says, holding her stomach, 'I like you, Jenna.'

My laughter subsides, and I hear her soft voice over and over in my head until I just sit there with satisfaction wrapping around me. *I like you.* That's what she said. *I like you, Jenna.*

Ethan's eyes are softer now, gently focused on mine, like the day I first saw him at the mission. 'Sorry,' he says. 'I didn't mean to be a dickhead.'

Dickhead? Another word I've lost. It must mean annoying or small-minded.

'I didn't notice,' I say, which brings another small chuckle from him.

'Dane pushes our buttons,' he says. 'Especially mine. Most of the time I try to ignore him.'

'We're different from others,' Gabriel says, like he is admitting something. 'But that doesn't mean we're freaks.'

'Dane has a way with words,' Allys adds.

Ethan swigs down a big gulp of milk and brings the bottle down like a gavel. 'Dane has a way with everything.'

'He keyed Ethan's truck last week,' Gabriel explains. 'No one can prove it, but weird things always seem to happen around Dane.'

'He's missing something. I mean, *really* missing something,' Allys says.

Gabriel shakes his head. 'He's not like us.'

'He's not like anyone,' Ethan says. 'That's probably why he's

78

in school with us. In that sense, he's right. We all have reasons for needing to come to a small alternative school. My theory is Dane's already been kicked out of every school within a thousand-mile radius.'

'At least,' Gabriel confirms.

I don't know what to say. They seem to be releasing every frustration they have about Dane, and yet I found him interesting. Blunt maybe, but something about him intrigues me. Maybe his honesty? He's the only one who bothered to tell me that I walk funny. Why didn't Claire? And what exactly is *funny*?

I'm glad when Allys turns the conversation from Dane to her. 'My reasons for coming to this school aren't so mysterious,' she says. 'A large campus just doesn't work for me anymore, and a flexible schedule makes therapy easier to work in. At an academy I would always be missing school. That's one of the reasons I'm here.' Allys picks up her sandwich and resumes eating. 'Plus, I like the course study better. Especially after all this'—she gestures with all four limbs. 'I have a particular interest in bioethics, and Rae lets me explore that. Why'd you want to come here, Jenna?'

'I didn't exactly want to. My mother chose it. I've been sick and . . .' I don't know how to finish. I still have a lightheaded aversion to saying the word *accident*. Has Mother drilled it into me that deeply not to speak about it? Or is there some other reason? But I don't want to lie.

'Accident,' I say much too loudly. 'I had an *accident*. And I'm still recovering.'

They all stare at me. My words have come out in halting spurts. *Lovely, Jenna.*

'You don't have to tell us—'

'And the worst part of it is, I've forgotten everything. I don't remember my parents, my friends, which things I love, and which things I hate. I can't even remember which side I parted my hair on—or maybe it was down the middle? And look at this,' I say, pointing at my legs. 'I obviously can't even remember how to walk!'

'It's okay—'

'It's all a blank. My life, my parents, my friends. I'm not sure I should even be here. I can't remember anything that matters,' I say in a desperate breathless finish, feeling like I have confessed a sin and I need forgiveness. Their forgiveness. Three friends. Are they friends?

Ethan's eyes, at that moment, are the kindest, deepest, safest brown I am sure I will ever know. I wait for him to absolve me of not remembering a mother who birthed me, a grandmother who saved me, friends who rebelled with me, and a suffocating fear I can't name.

'Jenna,' he says. His voice is as soft as a sparrow's beating wing, and I can almost feel the gentle flutter across my cheek. 'Thou speakest the loveliest ... load of crap.' He leans close and whispers, '*A single gentle rain makes the grass many shades greener. So our prospects brighten...*'

He waits expectantly. I lean in closer.

He watches my lips, and I let my words trickle out as softly as his. '*...on the influx of better thoughts. We should be blessed if we lived in the present always, and took advantage of every accident that befell us...*'

Ethan downs the rest of his milk. 'Two points made.'

'Three,' I say.

He raises his eyebrows.

'You're far more versed in *Walden* than you let on,' I say.

And not a dickhead at all, I think to myself.

Pieces

Isn't that what all of life is anyway?

Shards. Bits. Moments.

Am I less because I have fewer, or do the few I have
    mean more?

Am I just as full as anyone else? Enough?

Pieces.

Allys saying 'I like you'.

Gabriel snorting out bread, freeing me to laugh.

And Ethan reminding me how much I do know.

Pieces.

I hold them like they are life itself.

They nearly are.

Fine Tuning

'Don't forget, I'm coming home with Ethan,' I call out to the kitchen. 'So don't pick me up.'

I walk down the hallway, turn around, and walk back again, watching myself in the full-length mirror. I lift my feet carefully, but it seems overdone. Maybe it's my arms? Do they swing properly? I go back to the end of the hallway and try again.

Claire calls back, not to me but to Lily, loud so I can hear, 'Did you hear that, Mom? Jenna's coming home with *Ethan*. Sounds almost like a date.'

I smile. The last few days, Mother has been so cheerful, almost giddy that school has gone well. Perhaps she sees my life—and hers—coming back to us.

I stare at the mirror. I think it's my knees. I walk slowly, willing them into smooth movements. Better. I go to the kitchen. 'It's not a date, Mother. I'm just working at the Mission with Ethan until I find my own community project.'

Mother tilts her head and rolls her eyes. 'Oh. Sure. A community project. I've seen Ethan the last two days when I picked you up. He's—'

'Claire!' Lily yells. 'What's gotten into you? Do you really think it's wise to encourage this? Dating? Think it through!'

I glare at Lily. Mother and I are finally having something that resembles a conversation and she has to put a stop to it. Why does she have to be so annoying? So small-minded? So—

'Don't be such a dickhead, Lily!' I tell her.

Mother's jaw drops and she seems to forget what she was going to say.

Lily is silent for a moment and then bends over the counter. Laughing? *Is she laughing?*

I'm afraid I will never understand either one of them.

Jenna Fox / Year Fourteen

Since Lily isn't driving me to the mission until ten o'clock, I continue to fill the morning with the task of walking. I was hoping to have it figured out before I saw Ethan again. I practice in front of the mirror. I move slow. I move fast. I sway my hips, my hands, my chin. I glide, but it is all still off. I see that now. Am I trying too hard?

I decide to watch the videos. Maybe I'll learn something. Isn't that what Mother says? That it might trigger something? Maybe it will trigger something in my legs and arms so I walk like everyone else. I want to be like everyone else. I saw how Dane looked at me, before he saw me clod my way across the classroom. I liked the way his eyes were fixed on me. Close. Personal. So slow it almost felt like he was sliding his hands over me. It makes me feel different. Familiar. Maybe like the old Jenna.

'Play,' I say, and the disc follows my command.

I get lucky. Year Fourteen appears to be all about Jenna walking and moving.

As with all the discs, Year Fourteen begins with my birthday. I pose next to a street sign, Champs-Elysées, and then run along the street, the Arc de Triomphe as my destination. Paris. Not bad for a fourteenth birthday. 'Hurry, Dad!' I call. But I don't fuss too much. Jenna is so used to every move being recorded at this point that she seems to have surrendered herself to the adoration of Jenna Fox. There is no such thing as *hurry* for Mother or Father. I am too important. Why is this Jenna Fox so strong, but I feel less powerful than a single kilowatt?

Jenna stops on the sidewalk, a speck in the distance. She twirls, her arms outstretched, her face lifted to a blue and cloud-puffed sky, strangers passing her, absorbed in her perfect, happy world. Her movements are smooth and assured. Her limbs, graceful and elegant. Even her fingers look like calligraphy against the sky.

'Pause.' I stand and move to the center of my room. I stretch out my arms. I look at my fingers. They are every bit as lean and delicate as the ones on the disc. I turn. Slowly, at first. And then faster. I try to imitate fourteen-year-old Jenna, but my feet cannot keep up. My ankles collide. I stumble to the side and catch myself on my desk. Nothing has been triggered. I am still not the nimble Jenna Fox on the disc.

I look at my fingers again, the ones that trembled and shook just a few days ago at Mr Bender's kitchen table. I bring them together, fingertip to fingertip, like a steeple. Each one perfect in appearance. But something is not...right. Something that I still have no word for. It is a dull twisting that snakes through me. Is this a tangled feeling that everyone my age feels? Or is it different? Am I different? I slide my steepled fingers, slowly, watching them interlace. Trying to interlace, like a clutched desperate prayer, but again, I feel like the hands I am lacing are not my own, like I have borrowed them from a twelve-fingered monster. And yet, when I count them, yes, there are ten. Ten exquisitely perfect, beautiful fingers.

The New Lily and Jenna

Lily drives. I tap my knee. We don't speak. I watch her from time to time. Sideways, when I am sure she doesn't notice. I look at the lines fanning out from her eyes, the simple knot she has pulled her hair into, and the hastily placed clip that holds it together. She drives me to the mission because of Mother. I have figured that out now. Anything she does for me is really for Mother. There is nothing she wouldn't do for Claire.

They seem to be at odds right now over me. But I see the way Lily watches Claire, the way she will come up and squeeze her shoulders, or hug her for no reason at all, the way they still share something that I am not a part of.

I think she loved me once. But it is clear that is not the case anymore. She tolerates me. For Claire's sake, I gather. Occasionally she is touched by something in our past. I see a crack. Like the day I thought I was drowning. But then she puts her rigid exterior back on, like protection against me. Does she think I am dangerous? That I would hurt her?

Would I? I wanted to this morning in the kitchen when she told Claire to stop encouraging me. I think I wanted to hit her. Hard. I could have. But I didn't.

Strangely, I want her to like me. I don't know why. Maybe it is just wanting to go back to the way things were. To be the old Jenna. The one I don't know but the one she loved.

We take back roads. The hills are brown, dry, cold. But beneath the dry scruff, spring is emerging. Bright emerald grass contrasts with the brown chaparral that hovers above it. Winter is not welcome in California. It is only the beginning of February, and spring is already forcing its way in. Claire says she likes the temperate climate—that she will never go back to the icy winters again. That I will never go either. How does she know? I might. I will not always be seventeen.

We pass a toppled building, its rubble being eaten by weeds, and vines. Apparently after the quake, some parts of California were worth rebuilding and others were not. 'Hm,' Lily comments as we pass, forgetting our agreed silence.

'Are you afraid?' I ask.

She feigns surprise. 'Of earthquakes? No. When it's my time to go, I go.'

Is she really that confident? Just where does she think she's going? 'Go where?' I ask, enjoying pushing her.

She stares at me. Longer than is safe when driving fifty miles per hour. 'Never mind,' she answers and looks back at the road. I look straight ahead again, too. I know what *go* means to her, but I wanted her to say it.

Die.

Go.

To heaven? Is that where she thinks *she's* going? Is she really sure of going to a place that isn't even on a map? And how can she be sure she'd like it once she got there? But that's Lily. One big question mark.

We return to our silence. There are no more comments about tumbled buildings, who we are, were, or the strain between us. We return to something unnatural and painful and familiar. The way Lily and I are now.

The mission comes sooner than I think. We are here and I

long for more of the strained silence. It doesn't make sense, but I suppose in my new world, it does. I follow Lily down the same path as last time—through the heavy wooden gate, the cemetery, and finally through the church that leads to the inner courtyard where I am to meet Ethan. When she opens the door into the church, an unexpected wave of chanting stops us. A choir of pink-cheeked boys lift their voices as a priest seems to pull the music from their throats with the urging of his hands. Lily immediately crosses herself and closes her eyes. The echo of their voices makes me stop, too. It feels like it is shaking something inside of me, something that aches.

'Come along,' Lily whispers. 'They're practicing.'

We cross through the church, the priest acknowledging our presence with a nod but not stopping from his work. Lily opens the opposite door, and we exit to the courtyard.

'Ethan is bringing you home, so once I finish my business with Father Rico, I'll be going.' She turns to leave.

I am still filled with the sound of the boys' clear voices. I don't want to let it go. I don't want to let Lily go. She is already walking away. 'I heard you,' I say. She stops and turns around. 'Crying,' I add. 'When I was in a coma. I heard you cry out to Jesus. For me. I thought you should know. That people in a coma can hear.' Her fingers tighten around the bag in her hands. Her eyes are fixed on me, but she doesn't speak. 'Did you know I heard you?' I ask.

She opens her mouth, but her words seem to be stuck in her throat. 'No,' she finally says. 'I didn't know.' She swipes a strand of hair from her cheek. 'I need to go,' she says. 'I need to go.'

•   •   •

Ethan is not in the courtyard as promised, but after several misdirected attempts, I eventually find him at the lavanderia, the ancient washing basins next to the gardens. I don't even know what I will be doing for my community project. Rae just seemed to be satisfied that I could work with Ethan until I found a project of my own. We must devote eight hours per week to it.

'Finally,' he says when I arrive. But before he spits out his cold greeting, I catch something. A smile? Not so much around the mouth but in the eyes. I'm learning amazingly fast. He probably doesn't even know I saw.

'I got a lecture this morning, thanks to you,' I tell him.

'How so?'

'Apparently *dickhead* means more than annoying.'

'You called someone that?'

'My grandmother.'

He winces. 'You didn't know what it meant?'

'I told you, I've forgotten a lot—that's assuming I ever even had that lovely word in my vocabulary.'

He grunts and runs his eyes over me. 'I'm guessing you did.'

He wastes no more time on chat and shows me what is to occupy me for the next four hours. Dirt. I will be shoveling dirt spoonful by spoonful. The lavanderia is undergoing restoration to remove a thick layer of dirt that covers its northern end, brought about by some long-ago mudslide. The dirt must be removed carefully so as not to damage the ancient stones beneath it. We work side by side, using flat-bottomed trowels and occasionally shears to cut the vines and roots that weave through the blanket of dirt. I notice he works close by my side, even though there is a long wall of dirt to remove.

'So why is your grandmother a dickhead—I mean, annoying?' he asks.

I'm relieved that he breaks our silence first. 'Because she said we shouldn't be dating—' *Oh, my God, Jenna. Stupid. Stupid.*

'We're dating?'

'No. I mean, my mother thought—'

'Your *mother* thinks we're dating? Just because I'm giving you a ride home?'

'No. Well, yes. I mean, never mind.' *Help.* Every word seems to bury me further. Was I always this inept?

'Hm,' he says. He grins and stabs his trowel in for another load of dirt. We work for another silent few minutes shoulder to shoulder on our hands and knees, being careful not to dig too deeply, and then he sits back, resting one arm on his knee. 'So why doesn't your grandmother like me dating you, other than because I teach you bad words?'

I drop my trowel. 'We're *not* dating! And it's not you. It's me.'

'She doesn't like you? I thought grandmothers had to like you. It's a law or something.'

He's right. It should be a law. Or maybe it is for most people. Hearing him say it out loud makes it more painful. So obvious. Of course a grandmother should like you, and I wonder once again if Lily has good reason not to. Somehow, down deep, I think she does. I think of Kara and Locke. I ache for them. Does it have something to do with them? *Hurry, Jenna.* I hear their voices like they are whispering into my ear right now. I don't have a good response for Ethan. I feel like I should cry, but there are no tears. Not even a lump in my throat. I try to shrug off our conversation like it doesn't matter. 'I can't explain it. I guess I'm just special.'

Ethan looks at me like he is trying to decide something. His brown eyes make everything inside of me shift. He finally flicks some dirt from his fingers at me and smiles. 'Nah, Jenna. You're nothing special.'

In an instant, my insides swell, and I can't do anything but stand there returning his stare, and even though I should be embarrassed—*I am embarrassed*—I can't look away either. He moves first, awkwardly returning to his knees, and I join him, shoulder to shoulder, snipping, clearing, and scooping a spoonful of dirt at a time.

The sun is warm on my back. From time to time, I think I hear the chanting echoes from the church float on the breeze all the way down to the gardens, but Ethan says that is impossible. We are too far away. But I am sure I hear it. Or maybe the angelic tune is simply stuck in my head.

I decide I like shoveling dirt. I like the garden sounds and the mindless repetition. It is like it is the first time in weeks that my brain truly has been able to rest from trying to remember. For hours we work. Ethan stands now and then, stretching his back, rubbing his knees, but I don't tire.

'You're a horse,' he says.

'And you'—I want to find the right word—'are *not*.' Not much of a word, but the emphasis seems to have hit him nonetheless. He makes a show of rubbing his knees one last time and returns to my side. I smile, glad that my hair conceals my face.

Long stretches of time go by where we don't talk as we work. I listen to the birds in the garden, the chink of our trowels, the trickling of water from a nearby hose, and mostly to the voices in my own head. *You're fitting in, Jenna. You're loved, Jenna. You're normal, Jenna. You are almost whole, Jenna.* And mostly, I believe them.

'Do you know him?'

I glance to where Ethan is looking. At the top of the stairs that lead to the gardens, a squat man is watching us. Just as I look up, he clicks a picture and then walks away.

'No,' I answer. 'I've never seen him before.' Or maybe I have and I just don't remember him?

'Probably a tourist,' Ethan says. 'Usually they just visit the mission—not way down here. Or maybe Father Rico sent someone to check up on us.'

'Maybe,' I say.

Trigger

Sliding into Ethan's truck, I remember.

It's the gray leather.

I had a car.

But no license. I didn't have a license.

Mother and Father wouldn't let me get one.

Why would they give me a car

but not let me drive it?

I remember racing down the road in my car.

Hurry, Jenna.

I did.

And Kara and Locke were with me.

A Hundred Points

I slide across the seat of Ethan's truck to make room for Allys. We are picking her up from her community project before we head back to the village charter. We're outside the offices and labs adjacent to the Del Oro University Medical Center. Besides coming here for therapy, she also volunteers for the Del Oro Ethics Task Force. She gathers materials for review and helps process the numerous checks and balances that monitor their research activities.

'Grunt work,' Ethan called it when he described it to me. How could it be any more grunt work than spooning dirt? And I remember the way Allys spoke of it a few days ago. It's important to her. She is passionate, and I think she would do it even if Rae did not require a community volunteer project. She has accepted the loss of her limbs but blames an out-of-control medical system for the outcome. She thinks if someone had regulated antibiotics long ago, when they first knew about the dangers of overuse, she and millions like her would have had a different fate, and now she seems determined that no new medical injustices will be unleashed on the world.

When he talks about Allys, Ethan's voice takes on an edge I hadn't heard before. Like he feels her injustices, too. Does he care about her? How much does he care? Or does he have injustices of his own? I know nothing about him, really. Why is he at the village charter? Ethan said they all had their reasons for being there. Allys talked about her physical limitations. Gabriel said he had an anxiety disorder and the small environment was more comfortable for him, but Ethan never revealed his reasons.

'Can you take these?' Allys hands me the braces that still steady her, and she slides in next to me. 'Two more weeks, and these will be gone. At least that's what they tell me.' Her eyes sparkle, and her words come out in a continuous excited stream. 'They uploaded some new technology that will help the prosthetics anticipate my own balance system. It will supposedly read nerve signals from my brain and learn from them. They said to walk as much as possible to speed up the learning process. Imagine that—I've got smart legs.' She shoots a warning look at Ethan. 'Don't say a word.'

'Me?' Ethan says sweetly.

'I thought you were here for your volunteer project,' I say.

'That, too. But the therapy and the ethics offices are in the same complex, so I get it all done at the same time. How'd your project go?'

'Shoveling dirt?'

'She's a horse,' Ethan says, repeating his assessment of me.

'I liked it,' I tell her. 'It is not exactly a mental challenge—well, except maybe for Ethan—but Father Rico was very grateful.'

Ethan jogs the steering wheel to register my point, and Allys laughs. 'The mission's a good cause. They don't have funds, so without volunteers they'd never be able to keep it up. It has a lot of history that's important. It was my second choice right after the ethics office.'

'Who runs the ethics office? The hospital?' I ask.

'Are you kidding? The hospital hates the ethics office, but

they'd never admit it. You've never heard of the FSEB?'

I try to scan my pathetic excuse of a memory. It seems like I should know it. Like it is almost within my reach.

'It's not another bad word, if that's what you're thinking,' Ethan says.

'It's the Federal Science Ethics Board,' Allys says. 'They run the office. They're the yea and nay of all research and a lot of medical procedures, too. If you don't file all the forms and report every procedure, they shut you down. Whole hospitals. They've actually done it. Not often, but enough times that it's put the fear into every medical and research facility in the country.'

'Why do they do it?'

'They're the watchdog. There has to be some central control. Look at human cloning at the turn of the century. Even though it was illegal, some lab facilities were still doing it because the checks and balances were so weak. And then there's Bio Gel. That alone is probably responsible for Congress even establishing the FSEB.'

Allys is still talking, but it is a garbled echo. *Bio Gel.* Father's work. I can hear Lily saying it again, *He made a big splash.* 'Bio Gel?'

'It changed everything. It made almost anything possible.'

'What do you mean?' I ask.

Allys raises her eyebrows. 'You do have big blanks, don't you? Well, Blue Goo—as the hospital calls it—is, well, blue.'

'Brilliant,' Ethan interjects.

'And,' Allys says, raising her voice, 'it's artificially oxygenated and loaded with neurochips. They're smaller than the human cell and communicate with each other pretty much the same way neurons do, except faster. And they learn. Once you've loaded them with some basic information, they pass on information to other neurochips and begin to specialize. And of course, the truly spectacular thing is they can communicate with human cells in the same way. You pack a human or lab liver in Bio Gel, and the neurochips do the rest—deliver oxygen, nutrients, communicate with the central database, until it can be transplanted into someone who needs it.'

'Isn't that a good thing?'

'Sometimes. But just because we *can* doesn't mean we should. That's what the FSEB considers.'

'How so?' I ask, trying to sound only mildly interested.

'Well, one way is point values,' she says. 'Everyone gets a lifetime maximum of one hundred points. My limbs, for instance. The implanted digital technology to work with the prosthetics is very low point value. Sixteen points for all of them. But a heart— that's worth thirty-five alone. Throw in lungs and kidneys and you're at ninety-five points.'

'That sounds simplistic,' I say.

'Maybe. But fair, too. It doesn't matter how rich or important you are. Everyone's in the same boat. And medical resources and costs are kept under control.'

'What about brains?' Ethan asks. 'What are they worth?'

'Brains are pretty much illegal. Only biodigital enhancement up to forty-nine percent is allowed to restore some lost function and that's it.'

'That's an odd number,' I say. 'Why only forty-nine percent?'

'You have to draw the line somewhere, don't you? Medical costs are a terrible economic drain on society, not to mention all the ethics involved. And by restricting how much can be replaced or enhanced, the FSEB knows you are more human than lab creation. We don't want a lot of half-human lab pets crawling all around the world, do we? I think that's the main point of it all.'

'And the FSEB is always right?' Ethan asks.

Allys sits up straighter, and her words come fast and clipped. 'They're trying to preserve our humanity, Ethan. How can anyone argue with that? They're protecting us, and I for one think that is quite admirable. Plus, I happen to know there are a lot of very intelligent and qualified people in that agency.'

Ethan pulls into the parking lot at the charter. 'All I know is that a lot of "intelligent and qualified people" screwed up my life two years ago.' He throws the gear into park. 'So much for intelligence, huh?' It seems our conversation has taken a sudden turn that I wasn't expecting. Ethan's voice is rigid, like the day I called us all freaks at the market. He leaves to go into the charter, not waiting for us.

Allys lets out a huff of air. 'He can really go off sometimes.' She rolls her eyes and reaches for her braces. I watch him walk away, wondering if his life changed just about the same time mine did. And if, like me, he is still getting over it, though I don't know what the *it* is, and I'm afraid to ask. But I'm sure it's why he's at the charter now.

I wait outside for Ethan to take me home. I have already conferenced with Rae, and now Ethan's conference is going over.

'Hello.'

Dane surprises me from behind. I haven't talked to him much since that first day. He's been out. Rae didn't say why, and Mitch only groaned when Allys asked.

'How are things going?' His voice is warm and eager and I like the sound of it, but I also remember what Ethan said about him.

'Good,' I answer.

'Like your project?'

'Yes.'

'Need a ride?'

'No.'

He blows out a heavy breath, obviously annoyed at my short responses. He swings around in front of me and grabs my hand. 'C'mon. Has Ethan been saying bad things about me? You're not going to listen to him, are you?'

His hand is warm, firmly clasped around mine. I look up and am surprised at how closely his eyes match the color of the sky behind him. 'I have a problem,' he says. 'I admit it. I'm honest. Like when I said you walked funny. I don't think any less of you because you do, and I didn't mean anything bad by it. You're not going to hold that against me, are you?'

'No.'

He loosens his grip on my hand, but I notice he doesn't let go. 'We all have our problems, and Ethan's is he can't deal with the truth. He can't even tell the truth. I'd stay away from him if I were you, but I guess you'll figure that out on your own. You're obviously smart.' He smiles, but it doesn't mesmerize me like the day I first saw him at his house. I'm changing daily. I can see things in faces that I couldn't see just a few days ago. Things that I think other people can't even see. And what I see in Dane's perfectly beautiful face disturbs me. *Emptiness.* The word is strong in my head, and yet I wonder if it could be the wrong one.

'Friends?' he asks.

Friends. That's why I wanted to come to school in the first place. Maybe Dane had friends like I once did, friends who are gone now, and he misses them the way I miss Kara and Locke.

'Friends,' I repeat, because I know it would be rude not to. And because I think *maybe*. Maybe.

'Then I'll stop by sometime, since I just live down the street?' he says as he walks away.

'Sure.'

'Thanks for the invite, neighbor,' he calls over his shoulder.

Did I invite him?

Contents

> **Empty** adj. *1. Containing nothing, having none of the usual or appropriate contents. 2. Vacant, unoccupied. 3. Destitute of some quality or qualities.*

Now, a day later, I wonder what *friends* means to Dane. I wonder at his voice that is so different from his eyes. I wonder if I know anything at all. But I do know this: the word I felt when I looked into his face was the right word.

Home

The house is empty. Saturdays are empty, I decide. There is no banging. No restoration. No school. No anything. Mother left early in the morning. She didn't tell me where she was going but asked me to stay close by. I wanted to say no. But I didn't.

Lily's been out in her greenhouse all morning. She didn't invite me to join her. I wouldn't want to anyway. I've looked out my bedroom window twice, trying to see what she is doing, but most of the inside of the greenhouse is out of view. I don't care what she is doing.

I lie back on my bed and look at the ceiling. A Cotswold ceiling is fairly uneventful. It matches me.

Mother and Lily don't know, but Father was right. My memory is coming back.

It is curious how it comes. Each day, a rush of pieces, loosely connected, unimportant bits, snake through me. They click, click, click into my brain, like links being snapped together. And then they are done. A small chain of memories that fill in one tiny part of my life. They come out of nowhere, and most are not important.

I remember shopping for socks, feeling the socks, paying for the socks, looking at the receipt for the socks. Every detail of a sock-shopping outing that happened five years ago. Who cares about socks?

But then others... those come out of nowhere, too. Last night in the hallway, I was dizzy with the rush of this memory. I had to lean against the wall in the dark and close my eyes. It was so clear. I was sobbing. Screaming for Mother. I saw her crying. A tear, briefly, before she walked away. I cried for her to come back. I tried to reach out for her, but Father held me back. No. He held me. I was a toddler. Maybe eighteen months old.

I wore a bright red coat; Father, a black one. He kissed my

cheek. Wiped my tears. Promised she would return. I kicked my feet. He held me tighter. I remember it like it was yesterday. How can I remember this?

If I have to remember a lifetime of memories, bits at a time, will it take me another whole lifetime to reclaim them all? Or one day will they all connect up and explode inside of me?

I peek out my window again. No sign of Lily. The floor creaks beneath my feet. I walk to the other upstairs rooms. They are all still empty. Will Claire ever fill them? But with what? With only me? I go downstairs. I have never really properly explored the downstairs rooms. Other than a hurried rush to Claire's bathroom when I cut my knee, I have never spent any time in the rooms beyond the hallway. It only just now strikes me as odd that I have been like a houseguest, confining myself to my room and the shared rooms only, never feeling free to roam the rest of the house. *Stay close by, Jenna.* I am.

I go to the first doorway on the right in the downstairs hallway. Lily's room, I think. I push open the door, but it's an office. Claire's office, by the looks of the blueprints, fabric samples, and design books. It is cluttered and disorganized. Not what I would expect of Claire.

I move to the next doorway on the right. I turn the knob. The hinges squeal, startling me. Mother has still not updated the hardware and keys of the house. Maybe she thinks it makes the Cotswold more authentic, but it makes moving about unnoticed much more of a challenge. I find a large room, simply furnished. Yes, Lily's room. A pair of her shoes sits neatly in the corner. On the bureau is a scattering of framed pictures. Claire. My grandfather and Lily. And another one of a little girl in a pink party dress and black shiny shoes. A little girl who holds Lily's hand. The little girl Lily loved. I walk over and lay it facedown. So what if she knows. What can she do? Hate me? I feel empowered and I kick her shoes out of alignment, and I'm amazed that such a small action could feel so good. Enough of Lily's room for one day.

The next door on the left side of the hallway is locked. I move on to Claire's room. The master suite is large. Adjoining the bedroom is a sitting area furnished with two overstuffed chairs and a small library. An arched doorway on the other side of the bedroom leads to a dressing area, closets, and a bathroom. The closets form the same odd tunneling arrangement as mine does. Multiple closets for different needs. Overkill. The largest closet has another door at the back of it that leads toward the center of the house, so I know it would be a windowless room. I put my ear to the door and hear something. A faint hum. I jiggle the lever, but it is firmly locked.

The mattress. Mattress. Mattress. I walk to Claire's bed, throw back the bottom corner of the spread, and slide my hand beneath the mattress. I pull out my hand and try another corner. It is there. A key. I grab it and stand. For once I remember something about Claire that is useful.

'What are you doing?'

I slip my hand into my pocket. 'Nothing.'

'Looks like something to me.'

I look at the ruffled corners. 'I was just straightening Claire's bed. She left it unmade. There's nothing else to do around here.'

Lily looks into my eyes, like she's searching for something. I finger the key in my pocket, and she watches but doesn't say anything except, 'There's someone outside looking for you.'

I find Ethan on the front walkway. He shifts awkwardly and then smiles. He almost looks like he is in pain. 'Hello,' he says.

'Hello.' I look at him and wait, wondering what I am supposed to do.

'Oh!' He reaches into his jeans pocket and his strained smile vanishes. 'I found these keys in my truck. I thought they might be yours?' He holds out a ring with two card-keys dangling from it.

'No. Not mine.'

'Oh.' He doesn't move.

'Maybe they're Allys's,' I offer.

'Maybe.'

He shoves the keys back into his pocket, and the painful smile returns. 'I'll see you on Monday, then?'

'Your smile is so fake,' I say. 'You need more practice.'

His brows come together, and he snorts like he is offended. 'And of course you're the expert on smiles. Anything you don't know?'

'Not much.' I smile. Large and sustained.

He shakes his head and looks sideways at me. 'You win. I can't beat that.'

I ask him if he'd like a tour, and he says yes, he has nothing better to do. Nothing better? Yes, definitely Mr Personality. He seems interested in the new walkway the workers have laid and also in the dismantling and rebuilding of our chimney. When we walk around to the back, I see that Lily has returned to her greenhouse. I feel the key in my pocket. I could ask him to leave. This might be my only chance to be alone in the house for a long while. But I don't want him to leave. The key or Ethan. I choose Ethan for now.

We walk to the edge of the pond and he admires it. 'Not too many people have a pond in their backyard.'

I hadn't thought about it. We surely didn't have a pond in Boston. Ethan and I sit down opposite each other on a flat granite rock near the edge, and I appreciate the pond's beauty for the first time, seeing it through Ethan's eyes. Clusters of reeds shoot up like spiked anchors around the perimeter. On Mr Bender's side, some coot hens swim in and out of view between the cattails. 'I hear frogs at night,' I tell him. 'Even in February. Lily thinks it's strange.'

'Not so strange for here,' he says.

'Are you from here?'

He hesitates, looks at me like I have just asked him to give me a pint of blood rather than asked him a simple question. His answer is just as odd.

'Yeah.'

It is not the word, but the way it is said. Drawn out with a slight nod and a sigh. I recognize it. From somewhere. Maybe I saw it on Jenna's face or heard it in her voice on one of the video discs. A simple word that said more than was intended. *Resignation. Enough. Stop. What do you want from me?* Yeah. Things I think Mother never wanted me to see on those discs. Things that I think even the old Jenna never saw.

'*Here* is a problem for you,' I say.

'That's why I go to the charter,' he answers. 'A lot of people around here know me. It's easier there.'

'Because you can hide?'

'You put things together fast.'

'No. Not really. You said everyone has a reason for being at the charter. I was just waiting to hear yours.'

He leans forward, his arms resting on his knees. 'I spent a year in the state juvenile facility. I beat someone up. When I got out I couldn't go back to the academy, so I went to the charter.'

'You don't look the type,' I say.

'The type who would beat someone up until he's more dead than alive?' He looks past me, his eyes unfocused. I can hear the knot in his throat pulling tight. 'You just never know.'

I lean forward, my arms on my knees so our positions are mirror images of each other. *You never know.* Ethan knows more about himself than he ever wanted to know, and I know less than I should. It seems wrong that his dark past should elevate my own blank one. His eyes are dark, *full,* as full as Dane's are empty. I come forward so I am on my knees. So close to his face I should be embarrassed, but I'm not.

'Aren't you going to ask why?' he says.

I close the space between us. My lips on his, wondering if the old Jenna knew how to kiss and if the new one remembers, but judging by the way his lips feel against mine, the answer to both of my questions is yes. I finally pull back.

'Sorry,' I say. 'I should have asked.'

He pulls my face back to his and kisses me again, both of his hands soft against my cheeks.

Our kisses grow heated, and everything that is curious and odd and funny and wrong about me disappears and I am no longer thinking about me, but everything about Ethan, because the warmth of Ethan, the scent of Ethan, the touch of Ethan, is all about who I am *now*, and only when he pushes me away because Lily is yelling in the distance for me to come back to the house do I want to answer his question.

'I already know why. Because sometimes there is just no choice.'

Choice

I needed it like I needed air.
But no one could hear me.
No one could listen.
No words. No sound.
No voice.
I couldn't even dream myself away.
Choices were made.
None of them mine.
At first I wondered if it was hell.
And then I knew it was.

Message

I slam the kitchen drawer.

'It's not necessary to slam it. I already got the message that you're angry.'

I pull the drawer out and slam it again. I do it four more times. 'No! *Now* I think you get the message!'

'It *is* time for your nutrients.'

'Like you ever cared about that before!' I pull the bottle of nutrients from the refrigerator and pour the measured amount into a glass. When I put the nutrient bottle back in the refrigerator, I grab a container of mustard. I squeeze half of its contents on top of my prescribed beige brew. I glare at Lily, daring her to stop me, and I swig it all down. 'There! Done!' I slam the glass down on the counter, half expecting it to break.

'You shouldn't have done that. It might not . . . go down well.' She sighs like she is tired, and that makes me angrier.

'Why couldn't you just butt out like you always do?'

'It's not right, Jenna.'

'Says who?'

'Says everything in the universe.'

'I think he was enjoying it.'

'For now, maybe.'

I want to cry. I want to sob loudly. I want to beat something. Anything. I want to pound on her chest and say, *Please love me.* I want that minute back when I was kissing Ethan and now was all there was. I want someone in the world to answer why.

Why me?

And suddenly I feel weak, like every question in my head has collided against another and won't let me think. *Now* is the only word that comes out, and I know it makes no sense, but I say it again. 'Now.'

Lily's face wrinkles for a moment and then I see her hands stiffen, and the stiffness travels all the way to her mouth. She stands there staring at me like I have just recited a speech instead of one simple word. 'It's better this way,' she finally says. 'For Ethan and for you.' She leaves, and I hear her walk down the hallway to her room and close the door, and I wonder if she will even notice the down-turned picture or her out-of-place shoes.

Mustard and Kisses

It is only half past twelve, and I am already back in my room. My insides are shivery. I'm not sure if it is the half bottle of mustard I just swallowed or thinking about Ethan kissing me.

I don't care if the mustard goes down well or not. It was worth watching Lily stand there helplessly. She knew she couldn't stop me, and the little click of power that ran through me did go down well.

I scan my empty, no-personality room, and my gaze stops at my Netbook. I should watch another year of Jenna. Or learn more about my neighbors the way Mr Bender does. I feel like I should be doing something else. *Hurry, Jenna.* But instead I sit at my desk and lay my head down, wishing I could sleep and wake up a new me.

Sleep doesn't come. Neither does a new me. I stare at my

awkward monster fingers and feel my clumsy funny feet sliding back and forth on the floor beneath me, listening to the creaks and ticks of the house, and the heaves and sighs of restoration.

Jenna Fox / Year Sixteen

I place the last recorded disc of Jenna's life into the Netbook. What is there left to learn? I have more holes than substance, but I've pieced together a girl with the scatter of memories that have come back to me, and a life recorded beyond reason. I was treasured. Adored. Smothered with hopes. I was everything three babies could have been. I danced as hard as I could. Studied as hard. Played as hard. Practiced as hard. I pushed to be everything they dreamed I could be.

But with all the scenes, the birthdays, the lessons, the practices, the ordinary events that should have been left alone, what I remember most are Jenna's eyes, flickering, hesitation, an urgent trying. That's what I remember most from the discs, a desperation to stay on the pedestal. I see that in her eyes as much as I see their color. And now, in the passing of just a few weeks, I see things in faces I didn't see before. I see Jenna, smiling, laughing, chattering. And falling. When you are perfect, is there anywhere else to go? I ache for her like she is someone else. She is. I am not the perfect Jenna Fox anymore.

Like all the previous discs, this one begins with her birthday party, a lavish private affair somewhere in Scotland. Mother, Father, and I all wear kilts, and 'Happy Birthday' is played by a legion of bagpipers. The disc moves on to a school outing on a schooner. I scan the faces, looking for Kara or Locke. A few faces are familiar, schoolmates I remember, but not my friends, not the faces of my dreams. Where are they? Jenna's hair whips across her cheeks. She glances at the camera and for a moment becomes rigid, forcefully tilting her head sideways, silently pleading for space. Instead the camera zooms in. I can almost see her cave. Surrender. And then suddenly she runs. Weaving herself through the crowds of classmates. Away. And the camera shuts off.

Another scene begins. Jenna in pink tights, her hair pulled into a glittered bun.

'Give me a twirl, Jenna,' Father calls.

Claire comes into the room. 'Got everything? Shoes? Costume?'

'Yes,' Jenna says.

'What about that makeup?' Claire asks. 'A little overdone, don't you think?'

Jenna's eyes are heavy with eyeliner, dark smears that don't match her baby-pink tights. 'What difference does it make?'

'It might not please your ballet teacher.'

'I don't care if I please her. I told you, this is my last performance.'

Claire smiles. 'Of course it's not your last. You love to dance, Jenna.'

Jenna grabs Claire by both shoulders and looks down at her. 'Look at me, Mother. I'm five-nine and still growing. I'm not prima ballerina material.'

'But there are companies—'

Jenna throws her hands up. 'Why don't *you* be a ballerina! You're five foot seven, the perfect height! Go for it, Claire.'

I see Mother's face change. The hurt. I almost have to look away. Was that the first time I called her Claire?

'Ladies,' Father says. And the camera shuts off. That's it. The last recording of pre-coma Jenna Fox. A small argument with voices barely raised. Why would Lily suggest that this was the most important disc to watch? What was her point? The last disc is a non-event. Anticlimactic. Why did I think it would be something big? Or maybe she was just trying to save me hours of boredom? Cut to the end? See what a dickhead *I* was and get on with it. Move on. Maybe that's the something I feel. The something I should be doing. Moving on.

I've hurt Claire. I know that. I remember trying to tell her how sorry I was. When my whole world was frozen and *sorry* couldn't get past my lips. Sorry for what? The accident? All the harsh ways I treated her? Sorry for calling her Claire when she only wanted to be called Mom? Maybe that's why Lily won't have much to do with me, because of everything I've put Claire through.

Move on.

The something I should be doing.

Deep

Claire walks through the front door just as I reach the last stair. Her arms are loaded with rings of fabric swatches and catalogs.

'Need some help... Mom?'

She is transformed. One simple word has wiped five years from her face. I always thought it was Claire who held all the power. I was wrong.

I am taken with how beautiful she is and feel shame that I have withheld a treasured word for so long. She sets her armful down on the hall table. 'I can get it...Jenna.' Her voice is soft, my name sounding like a question mark.

I step down from the last stair. We stare, our eyes on an even plane, like we are holding something carefully between us. *Something*. Suddenly I feel dizzy, like I'm stumbling. Is this what moving on feels like? I back away. I can't do this. Something is not right. But I owe her. I know I owe her. My hands shake. My vision flashes. I try to steady myself. I shove my hands into my jeans. *The key*. It is still there. It is hot against my fingers.

'Do you mind, then, if I go for a walk? I've been inside all day.'

She hesitates, then nods. 'But don't go far,' she says as she walks to the kitchen.

When she is out of sight, I open the front door, then close it again, loudly, so she will think that I left. I concentrate on my feet, trying to step as lightly as I can, and I creep down the hall-way to her room. I will put the key back before she misses it.

I begin to fold back the spread from the corner of the mattress, but a thought stops me. *Hurry, Jenna*.

There might be time.

If I hurry.

I turn toward the closet and listen for sounds coming down the hallway.

None.

I pull the key from my pocket. It slides into the lock with a soft rasp, and I hear the tumbler turn. I ease the door open slowly, willing the old hinges not to squeak. The room is cold, dark, barely illuminated with a faint green glow. I feel for a switch but can't find one. My eyes adjust quickly to the dim light, and

I see the source of the hum. Computers. Three of them. They sit on a narrow table in the small dark room. They are oddly shaped, each a six-inch square block, much larger than a home computer, and each is connected to its own battery dock. Why not just run them off house power? I step closer and I see a small white label on the middle one.

JENNA ANGELINE FOX.

I rub my hand across the label, soaking the name in through my skin. Jenna *Angeline* Fox. I should have asked long ago. It makes me feel whole. A beginning, an end, *and* a middle. Why is it that the unknown is always so frightening? *Angeline.* I close my eyes in the darkness and whisper the name. I feel my feet on the floor, my place in the world. I belong here. I deserve to be here. How can a middle name do all that? Are the details of our lives who we are, or is it owning those details that makes the difference?

I open my eyes and examine my computer. I wonder what's on it. Schoolwork? Letters to friends? I feel a surge, like a jolt of energy has shot through me. History. *My history.* It should be in *my* room. I try to lift it from the table, but it is secured with a metal bracket. I work to pull it loose. One rivet pops out, but the rest stay secure. I pound at the bracket with the heel of my hand, throwing the full force of my weight behind it, but my hand slips and slices into the sharp edge. Pain rips up my hand and I fall back, but just as quickly the pain is gone. I hug my hand to my stomach, afraid to look. I know the slash is deep. If Mother had a meltdown over the tiny cut on my knee, I can't imagine what she will do when she sees this one.

A trickle of blood oozes through my fingers. I will have to retrieve my computer later. I step out of the closet, lock it, and hurry to my room, trying to slip silently upstairs. I go to my bathroom and lock the door behind me.

How bad could it be? It was only a little piece of metal. I hold my hand over the sink to spare the floor, but thankfully the blood has already stopped flowing. A three-inch gash runs from the fleshy part of my thumb to my wrist. I am surprised that it no longer hurts. Will I need stitches? I pull the flesh apart to see how deep the wound goes.

It is deep.

What. How.

Oh, my God.

I can't. Think.

Deep.

Blue

The stairs rock. Sway.

I clutch my gashed hand to my stomach. The other gropes at the stair rail.

Only a small smear of blood stains my shirt. So little. And it is barely red. Is it red at all?

My feet stumble on the stairs, and I fall down three at a time.

'Jenna?' A distant call from the kitchen.

More stairs. And no pain. My hand doesn't hurt.

The hallway rocks and the doorway sways. Mother and Lily are framed in light at the kitchen table.

They stop their conversation. Stare at me. Mother focuses on my shirt. The bloodstain. She begins to rise, but a single word from me stops her.

'When?'

'Jenna—'

'When were you going to tell me!' I yell. I shove my hand out in front of me. *'What is this?'*

Mother's hand comes to her chin, half covering her mouth. 'Jenna, let me explain—'

Lily rises. 'You should sit down,' she says. She steps behind her own chair and offers it.

I sit down because I don't know what else to do. I look up at Claire. 'What's wrong with my hand?' I lay it on the table and spread the gash apart with my fingers. The skin lies on a thick layer of blue. Blue gel. Beneath that is the silvery-white glimmer of synthetic bone and ligaments. Plastic? Metal composite? Mother looks away.

'What happened?' I ask. My voice is a whisper.

'It was the accident,' she says.

The accident. 'Was it cut off?'

Mother reaches out. She lays both of her hands on my arm. 'Jenna, darling.'

'Tell me.'

'It was burned. Terribly burned.'

I look at my other hand resting on the table next to the gashed one. *My other perfect hand.* The perfect hand that won't lace right. The monster hand. I look at Mother. She looks like she is crumbling inward, caving like a terrible weight is pressing on her. 'What about . . . *this* one?' I ask, raising my other hand.

She nods.

Oh, my God. I look down, the world disappearing beyond the circle of my lap. I am suddenly so cold. My skin that has never felt right instantly feels foreign. I hear Lily move to the other side of the table. The scraping of a chair. The sigh as she sits. It all pounds in my ears. My hands twitch. I look at them. Can I even call them *my* hands?

I turn to Mother. 'Is there anything else?'

The tears flow. Her face is desperate. 'Jenna, what difference does it make? You're still my daughter. That's all that matters—'

My clumsy feet. My legs.

Oh, God no.

'Stand up,' I say. I rise to my feet. Mother looks at me, confused. 'Stand up!' I yell. She stands, inches from me. We look eye to eye. We are the exact same height. 'How tall are you, Mother?' I whisper each word distinctly, like a string of knots in a rope I am clinging to.

'Jenna?' She doesn't understand. She doesn't know what I've seen. In the last video that Lily told me to watch, where I blurt out my height. Fear twists her face. She doesn't answer.

'How tall are you?' I demand.

'Five-seven.'

I collapse back into my chair, shaking my head. Mother is mumbling, rambling, saying something that is all noise for me. I finally force myself to look at her. 'Tell me everything.'

'What?' she says, pretending she doesn't understand what I'm asking. She does. I see it in her eyes, a frantic back-step, hoping all this will go away.

'How much is me?'

Her lip trembles. Her eyes pool.

Lily intervenes. 'Ten percent. Ten percent of your brain. That's all they could save. They should have let you die.'

I try to understand what she is saying. I watch her mouth move. I hear words. Ten percent. *Ten percent.*

And then Mother is suddenly fierce. A lion. Within inches of my face. 'But it is the most important ten percent. Do you hear me? The most important.'

Pinned

I lie in my bed. I stare at the ceiling. Claire paces. Leaves. Comes back. Pleads. Informs. I listen but I don't respond. Lily comes in, too. Watches. Whispers to Claire. Steps closer to me. Leaves. And comes back.

They don't know what to do with me. Father is coming. Claire called him. Hours ago. It is now the middle of the night. Two A.M. He will explain it all, Claire says. When he gets here. He will make me understand. And yet she sits on the edge of my bed and tries to explain herself.

'You were burned so badly, Jenna. We tried everything. Even with all the temporary grafts, you were losing so much fluid. We had you stabilized for a few days. I was so hopeful. But then the infections set in and we were losing you fast. The antibiotics weren't working. There wasn't time for a lot of decisions. Your father pulled me into a closet, Jenna. A closet! *That's* where we had to decide. He whispered to me the only possible way of saving you. We had to make a choice—save you the only way we knew how or let you die. Any parent in the world would have made the choice we did.' Her hands knead the side of my bed. She stands. Circles my room. Returns to the end of my bed.

'We had you moved. Immediately. To a private facility. A private room. All physicians on your case were dismissed, except for the ones who worked with your father at Fox BioSystems. The infection was moving so rapidly through you. Your father actually injected you with the nanobots while you were in an ambulance en route to the new facility. They had to start the brain scan right away.'

'Why?'

She stands again. Her face is alert. Careful. Bright. She is encouraged that I spoke. She shouldn't be.

'Your veins were collapsing. We weren't sure how much longer your heart could last. Blood circulation is critical for a good scan. They take at least six minutes. Vital organs were already shutting down. By the time they got you to surgery, your heart had stopped twice. They had the Bio Gel waiting. They saved as much as was still viable.'

She comes close. White. She falls to her knees beside my bed and takes my gashed hand in hers. She holds it like it is keeping her from dissolving away. 'The butterfly, Jenna. That's what they call it. The heart of the brain. That you still have.'

And the rest. My memories? My history? Those aren't all in the butterfly. What is the rest? How am I remembering so many things? Nearly everything now. Except the accident.

I close my eyes. I want her to go away. I don't want to talk about butterflies or hearts. I don't even want answers. I don't want *her*. I feel her cheek against my hand. Her breath. Her need. And then she slowly lets go and leaves.

I open my eyes again. My room is dark. The silence of the house is a heavy blanket. It pins me to my bed.

White

There was a moment in the darkness when the fear lifted.

A moment where white surrounded me.

Hope.

Lily, and someone else, and a sprinkling of water.

'Holy water, Jenna.'

'You can let go if you need to.'

'Forgiveness, Jenna.'

But I couldn't let go.

It wasn't in my power.

I was already swirling, flying, falling.

To someplace deep I didn't understand.

Where all the sounds but my own voice disappeared.

Only me.

For so long.

I don't want to be alone anymore.

Father

I hear a creak. My clock reads three A.M. Father stands in my doorway, the soft yellow light from the hallway illuminating his face. A shadow of stubble is on his cheeks. His hair is uncombed. His eyes are hollow. He looks like he could have run here all the way from Boston.

'Angel,' he whispers.

'I'm awake,' I say.

He comes in and sits on the edge of my bed. 'I'm sorry,' he says. 'I didn't want you to find out this way.'

'My hands are artificial,' I tell him. 'My legs, too.'

He nods.

I sit up and lean against the headboard of my bed. I lift my hands in front of me and stare at them. 'I loved my hands. My legs.' I say it more to myself than to him. 'I had never thought about it before. They were just there. And now I can see that these'—I turn them, looking at the palms—'these are different. They're not mine. They're imposters.'

I wait for him to deny it, to erase the last twelve hours with just a few words. I watch his face. Even in my shadowed bedroom I can see how tired he is. I can see the red rims of his eyes. 'They're nearly identical to the original,' he says. 'All of your ballet recital videos allowed us to digitally measure every centimeter of you.'

'Hurray for videos, huh?'

He hears the sarcasm in my voice and closes his eyes momentarily. I ache. Maybe for his pain. For Claire's. But mostly for mine. My loss. I can't care about theirs. Not now. How did I get to this point? How can I go back?

He takes my hand in his and examines the gash.

'It's not even real skin, is it?' I say.

'Yes. It's real. Some of it is even yours.'

'How?'

'It's lab skin. Grown in the lab and genetically engineered to be nourished through the Bio Gel. It took months to get all the skin types we needed. We could only harvest a small portion of yours because of the burns and infection. But still, we did get some.' His voice is stronger, less tired. He is more confident as a doctor than as my father.

'What do you mean, engineered?'

'We had to make some changes so nutrients and oxygen could be delivered in a modified way.'

'So it's not human skin.'

'It is human. Completely human. We've been genetically altering plants and animals for years. It's nothing new. Tomatoes, for instance. We engineer them to withstand certain pests or to give them a longer shelf life, but it is still one hundred percent a tomato.'

'I am not a tomato.'

He looks at me sharply. 'No. You're not. You're my daughter. You have to know, Jenna, I would do anything to save you. You're my child. And I want to be honest with you. So let's cut the crap. Lab skin is yesterday's news. You want to know more than that. Let's move on.'

I always loved that about Father. He was direct. Claire and I could dance around a subject for days and weeks. But not Father and me. Maybe because he was around less. He didn't have time to dally. Right now I want to dance. I feel like I could dance forever.

'Jenna,' he says, nudging me.

'Skin, bone, that's one thing,' I say. 'But Lily says you only saved ten percent of my brain. True?'

'True.'

'Then what am I?'

He doesn't hesitate. 'You're Jenna Angeline Fox. A seventeen-year-old girl who was in a terrible accident and nearly died. You were saved the way so many accident victims are saved, through medical technology. Your body was injured beyond saving. We had to patch together a new one. Your skeletal structure was replicated. You have all the bone structure of a normal teenage girl. Muscle areas are taken up with additional modified Bio Gel. Most movement is accomplished through digital signals within the bone structure. Some is accomplished through the traditional method of cabled ligaments. Your skin was replaced. Your brain, the ten percent we saved, was infused with additional Bio Gel. But obviously ten percent is not enough for full function, so we scanned your whole brain and uploaded the information for safekeeping until we had the rest of the elements in place—'

'Uploaded? You uploaded my brain?'

'The information. Every bit of information that was ever in your brain. But the information is not the mind, Jenna. That we've never accomplished before. What we've done with you is groundbreaking. We cracked the code. The mind is an energy that the brain produces. Think of a glass ball twirling on your fingertip. If it falls, it shatters into a million pieces. All the parts of a ball are still there, but it will never twirl with that force on your fingertip again. The brain is the same way. Illegal brain scans have been going on for years. Nanobots the size of blood cells are injected, sometimes even without a person's knowledge since it's all wireless transfer. Bits of information are extracted. But the mind, *the mind* could never be transferred. It's an entirely different thing from bits of information. We found that it's like a spinning glass ball. You have to keep it spinning or it falls and shatters. So we upload those bits of information into an environment that allows that energy to keep spinning, so to speak.'

'To keep *thinking.*'

He nods.

That environment was my hell. My black void I didn't understand. My endless vacuum where I suffocated, screamed, cried, but no one came to help me.

My own father put me there.

I lay my face in my hands. The hands that are not really mine. I suck in a ragged breath. Do I even have lungs, or is this just a remembered action? I shudder, repulsed at everything that I may or may not be, wanting to escape but trapped again. By what? Myself? I don't know who or what I am anymore.

I feel Father's arms around me. His stubble scratching my cheek. Whispering in my ear, 'Jenna. Jenna. It will be all right. I promise.' He is my father again, not the doctor. The confidence is gone. I hear the fear in his voice. He is not sure things will be all right.

I push him away. 'I need to know. Everything.'

'You will. But even that ten percent needs rest. Let's both get some sleep. We'll talk more in the morning.'

I am tired. Drained. I nod and I lie back on my pillow.

Just before he reaches the door, I stop him. 'Is it true?'

'True?'

'Is there really a most important ten percent?'

'Yes,' he says. 'I truly believe there is.'

Day One / New Jenna

Father staples my skin together. I feel a quick pinch.

'It's deeper than I thought it was last night,' Father says. 'How did you do this?'

'It happened when I—' *Careful, Jenna. They hid your computer from you.* 'It happened when I went for a walk. I stumbled and came down on a rock.'

'A rock did this?'

'It had a sharp edge to it.'

'Oh.' I am not sure he believes me, but then again, I am not sure how much to believe of what he says either. I guess that makes us even. He swabs the now-stapled cut with gel and begins wrapping it with gauze. We sit at the kitchen table. Claire, too. She is still in the clothes she had on yesterday, rumpled now. Her usually neat hair is uncombed. She is tired, her face looking numb, like she has no energy to express anything, but still I can tell she is restraining herself from talking; she is letting Father do most of it. He holds nothing back, and I see Claire wince at some of the information.

'If I only have ten percent of my original brain, what is the rest?'

'It's not exactly correct that you don't have your brain. You do. You just don't have the same material it was housed in. Now it's in the Bio Gel.'

'Then explain Bio Gel.' I ask my questions flatly. Not committing to emotion. Not angry. Not sad. Not committing to acceptance or forgiveness. I can't give them that.

'Bio Gel is an artificial neural network built on a biological model. It's a condensed, oxygenated gel that is filled with neural chips. These chips are as small as human neurons, and the wonderful thing is, they communicate and pass messages in the same way human neurons do, through chemical neurotransmitters. The typical human brain, Jenna, is composed of a hundred billion neurons. You have *five* times that. Every inch of you is packed with Bio Gel.'

I sense that Father thinks I should be impressed. Maybe even grateful. But what about my missing heart? My liver? I don't want five hundred billion neural chips. I want guts.

He continues to describe his handiwork. 'We uploaded all the information from your brain to a central sphere around your saved brain tissue—the pons—or the butterfly as it's sometimes called. But eventually all the information will be shared with the whole network.'

'If it's all there, why am I having a hard time remembering?' I don't share that there are some things I am remembering that I shouldn't. Like my baptism at two weeks old. I want to believe that Father has it all under control, but memories like these tell me he may be as lost as I am. He's tampered with the unknown. What door has he opened? Will he change his mind and want to close it?

'Your memory lapses aren't unlike someone who's had a stroke and is slowly recovering,' he says. 'The brain has to find new pathways to access and store information. That's what you're doing now. The neural chips are building pathways.'

'Are you sure it's all there?'

Mother and Father share a quick glance. Do they think I am blind?

'Reasonably sure,' Father says.

Reasonably. Like that is enough.

Father is done with my hand and I stand. 'So if this is all so groundbreaking and wonderful, why are we here?' I know the answer, but I want to push them—like a child on a playground shoving at someone's shoulder. It feels good. I answer my own question before they can put their spin on it. 'I'm illegal, aren't I? That's why we live here. We're hiding out.'

Mother stands, coming around the table toward me. 'Jenna, the laws will change—'

Father jumps in. 'You've done nothing wrong. What *we've* done is illegal. So, yes, that's one of the reasons we're here.'

Mother is about to reach me, and I put my hand out like a stop sign to halt her. '*One* of the reasons?' I ask.

Father hesitates. Another shared glance between him and Mother. 'The Bio Gel has its limitations. We know the shelf life— the oxygenation—is reduced with extreme temperature changes, especially cold. This location was chosen because it has the most constant temperate climate in the country.'

I begin laughing. *Shelf life?* My God, I have a shelf life!

'It's not that unusual—'

'Stop! I have a shelf life, for God's sake! That *is* unusual!'

'Call it whatever you want, but what living thing doesn't have a shelf life of some sort? We all do. You're twisting this out of—'

'I can't believe this!' I circle around, my arms flailing over my head, but just as quickly I'm disgusted that I'm mimicking Claire's nervous gestures. I stop cold and face Father. 'How long does it last?'

'In this environment, we think it may have a good two hundred years. The problem is, there is no data yet—'

'And if I were to go to a cold climate? Boston?'

'Again, we don't have definitive data, but it could be reduced to just a couple of years or maybe even less.'

I stare at them both. Just when I thought it couldn't get worse, it does. I have a life expectancy between two and two hundred years. What's next? I back toward the door. 'How could you do this to me?'

'We did what any parent would do. We saved you.'

'Saved what? I'm a freak! You saved an uploaded artificial freak!'

Mother steps closer and in an instant her hand shoots up ready to slam across my face, but she catches herself, her hand frozen in midair. She deliberately lowers it to her side. Even in her rage, she cannot harm one cell on her treasured Jenna's face. 'Don't you dare call yourself that! And don't you dare judge us! Until you've been in our shoes, you'll never understand!' She turns abruptly and leaves the room.

Father and I stare at each other. Her exit leaves a hole, an imbalance to our already teetering triangle.

'It's been very difficult for her, Jenna,' he finally says, his voice soft and uneven. Is he unraveling, too? They're both disintegrating before my eyes. I need to get out. *Get away, Jenna.* I open the kitchen door to the backyard and step halfway out—*like it hasn't been hard for me?* I turn and look at Father again.

'I'm illegal. No matter how you play with the words...*I'm illegal.* I don't even know if I'm human.'

Father collapses into a chair. He leans forward, his fingers digging across his face and scalp. 'I do know. You are one hundred percent human.'

'How can you be sure?'

'I'm a doctor, Jenna. And a scientist.'

'Does that make you an authority on everything? What about a soul, Father? When you were so busy implanting all your neural chips, did you think about that? Did you snip my soul from my old body, too? Where did you put it? Show me! Where? Where in all this groundbreaking technology did you insert my soul?'

I turn and leave before I can hear his answer. If he had one.

Lily

I was always bright. I always got As. But I wasn't smart like Kara and Locke. They were truly brilliant. More than just book smart. It wouldn't have taken them this long to catch on.

I sit on the large flat rock that just yesterday Ethan and I kissed on. Yesterday when I was only a girl with a shaky memory. Yesterday is a world away now.

I was going to run into the woods, out of view, but I know they would panic. Maybe even follow me. What might happen to their precious Jenna? They're probably watching me now. From a window. Wondering. Ready to pounce. Second-guessing every thought I might have. Wondering if they could have done something differently. Wondering what they should do next. I can almost feel their eyes on my back. I whip around, but all I see is a cold, silent house. Bricks sit in pallets, waiting to repair the veranda. Scaffolding for painters stands empty. All workers have been turned away today. Restoration is on hold.

I haven't seen Lily at all. We all need space.

I stare at the pond. It is mostly still. A coot hen on Mr Bender's side disturbs the water every few minutes, diving for something on the bottom. The ripples don't even reach our side of the pond. They disappear somewhere in the middle. I concentrate on that short expanse, where something becomes nothing. Exactly when does it disappear? And where does it go?

I pull my sneaker off and throw it as far as I can. It splashes into the middle of the pond, and the coot hen is startled into the reeds. Ripples fan out. They reach both shores, but within a minute the surface is glass again, the sneaker's splashy entrance forgotten, and I am minus a shoe. It is the least of my worries, and now I am back to that. Me. Or whatever I am.

My own question to Father has caught me by surprise. There is no going back. Where did the question come from? Were my artificial neural chips begging me to recognize what was left behind? Was it? It burrows into me, like a foxtail inching into flesh.

My soul.

I pull my sock from my sneakerless foot. It looks like real flesh. Real toes. Ally's prosthetics are well made, but they are clearly not like this. These are real. They feel. I skim my foot out along the rock, feeling the cold surface, the uneven granite. Bits of grit.

I stare at the once again glassy surface of the pond. I curl my toes against the rock. I listen to my toenails scratching the stone. Digging. Chipping. The questions circle back. *Is there such a thing? Was mine left behind?*

I look at my hand curled in my lap, the bandage now covering the secret. The sick feeling of when I first saw it returns. In one moment, one brief glance, reality can flip. Whatever we believe can vanish. Believing in something doesn't make it so.

There were so many things Mother and Father always wanted me to be. But wanting didn't make it so, either. Now they want me to be just who I was before. I'm not. No matter how much they want it, or how much I want it, I can't make that happen. The feeling of failure is familiar. I always tried so hard to be everything they wanted. Everything three babies could be. Their miracle child. Me. Now I am a different kind of miracle. The artificial freak kind.

'The world has sure changed, hasn't it?'

I startle and turn around. It is Lily. I didn't hear her come up behind me. I turn back without answering.

'Mind if I sit down?'

I stare out at the pond, silent, and hug my knees to my chest. She sits down, uninvited.

The rock is large. The distance between us small. I feel every inch of it. The lack of conversation doesn't seem to bother her. It suffocates me. She is here for a reason. What is she waiting for? She finally breaches the wall of quiet between us. 'I'll be honest. I don't really know what to make of you.'

I smirk. It is close to a laugh. She never lets up. But somehow I can accept her bluntness more easily than lying. 'You don't tiptoe, do you?'

'What would be the point?'

'Right,' I say, still staring straight ahead. 'Why spare any feelings when the feelings belong to a freak?'

'Your words. Not mine.'

'Some things don't have to be said out loud.'

'Eighteen months ago, I let go of my granddaughter,' she says. 'I said good-bye. I grieved. Then a few hours later, your parents told me what they had done.'

'And you thought it was wrong?'

'I'm not like your parents. I think there are worse things than dying.'

I think of the dark place, where I was nowhere at all. Trapped, dead, but alive. I hug my knees tighter and turn my face to look into Lily's eyes that have been watching me all along. 'And that's what you think Jenna did? Died?'

She shakes her head. 'There you go again. Putting words in my mouth. You were always good at putting—' She stops abruptly, like she has caught herself admitting to something. 'Like I said before, I didn't know what to make of you. That's all.'

'Didn't. Don't. Which is it?'

'What?'

'Two different things. First time you said you don't know what to make of me. Just now you said didn't. Past tense. Big difference. You've come to a decision?'

She laughs. 'God, you sound like Jenna. You look like Jenna. You can even be so damn precise and picky and aggravating like Jenna.'

She begins to reach out like she is going to touch my knee, but then she pulls back and returns her hand to her lap. 'I just don't know if you're a perfect replica of my Jenna, or—'

'Or the miracle you prayed for?'

She nods, her lips tight. My nana. I lay my head down on my scrunched-up knees and close my eyes, even though I loathe the darkness.

'I don't know either,' I say. I speak the words into the dark, crowded angles of my folded arms and legs. I'm not even sure she can hear me. Or if anyone can. It's a familiar feeling I never wanted to return to.

Species

> **Human** n. *1. A member of the species* Homo sapiens.
> adj. *2. Representative of the sympathies and frailties*
> *of human nature. 3. Sympathetic, humane. 4. Having*
> *human form or attributes.*

Where do I go from here?

How many hours can one person spend locked in a bathroom, looking at skin, hair, eyes. Feeling fingers. Toes. And the absurdity of a belly button?

How many definitions for *human* can one person find? And how do you know which one is correct?

How many hours can you spend shivering? And holding.

And wondering.

Details

We sit in the living room. Father builds a fire, even though Mother warns that the top of the chimney is still missing. He doesn't care. He wants a fire. If the house burns down, he'll build another. She doesn't argue.

His time here is limited. He will be missed in Boston. Questions will be asked, and the others can't cover for him for long. So in this unplanned visit he tries to tell me more of what I need to know. At dinnertime I learned more about the new and improved Jenna. Even though Bio Gel is self-sufficient, I actually do have a primitive digestive system, mostly for 'psychological reasons'. No stomach, but an intestine of sorts. It explains my infrequent trips to the restroom and unusual constitution. And the system does utilize the nutrients for my skin. At some point, I may be able to eat some table foods. I tell Father I have already indulged in mustard and he frowns, but he doesn't say anything. It's like he can't take any more drama. Even if it may derail everything he and Mother have worked toward for so long. Mustard. Irrelevant.

Mother has been mostly quiet. Before dinner she apologized for raising her hand to me. She stumbled over her words. I don't recall her ever hitting me, but even the possibility seems to shake her. Now she sits in the wingback chair near the fire, her head back, her eyes staring at something I can't see. The past? Is she retracing every moment, wondering what she should have done differently? Always chatty and in control, she is now the opposite, like someone has pulled her plug. Father fills the space she leaves by adding logs in the fireplace and refilling both their brandy glasses. I have never before seen Mother drink anything stronger than cranberry juice.

Father doesn't address the question I threw at him before I ran out the kitchen door this afternoon. Perhaps, like mustard, it is irrelevant to him. I don't think it is irrelevant to Lily. She had been conspicuously absent all evening. She helped make dinner but didn't join Mother and Father in eating it, instead excusing herself and going to her room. 'You need some time alone together,' she said.

As he pokes at the fire, Father explains in detail more than I really want to know the tedious process of saving bits of my skin and growing it in the lab and combining it with other specimens until the required amount was achieved. He moves on to the technology of brain scans, what he and his team have learned just from my experience and the implications for future patients facing similar problems. As long as he is in doctor-scientist mode, he is talkative and in charge. When he veers into father mode, he stumbles and looks in many ways like a mirror image of Mother. He ages. Who is this Jenna Fox who has so much power over them? I feel like a weak, unsure ghost of her. Maybe a replica. I search for some portion of her strength.

Father leans back in a chair opposite Mother and talks of the challenges of uploading. I am poised on the middle of the sofa between their chairs. The scientific complexities don't matter to me as much as the human ones do. When will we talk about that?

I cut into his safe, doctor mode.

'Why didn't you tell me?' I ask. 'The minute I woke up? Didn't I deserve to know?'

His head drops momentarily. His chest rises. Mother's eyes close. 'Maybe we should have, Jenna,' he says. He stands and paces near the hearth. 'I'm not saying we did everything right. Damn, it's not like there's a manual for this sort of situation. We're groping our way through this. It's a first for us, too, just like it is for you. We're—'

He stops his pacing and looks at me. 'We're just doing the best we can.' I hear the catch in his voice, and it knifes through me.

Mother opens her eyes and the lioness returns. They are a tag team. When one is spent, the other takes up the fight. 'We know this is hard on you, Jenna. It's hard on us, too. Someday you'll understand. Someday, when you have a child of your own, you'll finally understand what a parent will do to save their child.'

'*Look at me!* I can never have a child!'

She softens. 'We saved an ovary, darling. It's preserved at an organ bank. And a surrogate mother won't be a problem—'

God! Bits of me have landed everywhere. It would be funny if it wasn't so horrifying. I stand abruptly, judging whether to leave or stick it out. 'Please, can we stay with one issue at a time? I asked a simple question,' I say. 'Why didn't you tell me? You didn't forget. I remember that much about both of you. Details don't escape you. I've lived with details for years.' I look directly at Claire. 'I won't even bring up the fact that I am two inches shorter now—acceptable ballerina height—another detail I know wasn't an oversight. So let's just go back to my original question. What took you so long?'

'Listen very carefully,' she says. Her face and voice are hard. 'Every ounce of our breath was sucked out of us. For days we didn't breathe. Literally, *that's* what it felt like. And every time I looked at you, I was afraid to look away again, like my eyes were the only thing anchoring you to this earth. It was unbearable every time I looked at you, but I couldn't look away either. So, if we didn't do everything just right, understand it's not just *you* who's been through hell.'

Stalemate. It's true. I read it on their faces. The years and the lines I've added.

'But you're right. There's more,' she adds. 'It doesn't matter anymore, but weeks ago we couldn't tell you because we weren't sure what your mental state would be. Judgment, specifically. There are a lot of people who have laid their lives and careers on the line for you, Jenna. We had to be careful. If you slipped and told someone, you would not only jeopardize your future but theirs as well.'

How can I argue with this? But how can I handle any more weight of being the perfect Jenna, now not just for Mother and Father, but for people I don't even know? When does it end? I lean my forehead against the mantel and close my eyes.

'And for the record,' Father says, 'your mother had nothing to do with your being two inches shorter. It was a decision based on mechanics, ratio, and the limitations of balance. A few inches shorter would have been even better, but two was the perfect compromise.'

Perfect. A shorter, more perfect Jenna. How wonderful.

Careful, Jenna.

There's still more. It speaks to me. Somewhere, winding inside, pieces are trying to come together, synapses trying to form, a complete story trying to connect within. Four hundred billion extra neural chips trying to put together what the old Jenna never could.

Mother's hand is on my shoulder. 'Please, for all our sakes—especially yours—you mustn't say anything to anyone.'

I nod, unable to speak. Father reaches out. He pulls me close, squeezing, and I melt into his shoulder, letting his arms circle me like a warm, tight blanket.

Hold On

'Do you hear me, Jenna?
I'm here. I won't let you go.'
I dreamed I was riding my bicycle. My first two-wheeler,
    the training wheels gone.
But Father's voice was all wrong.
'Hold on, Jenna. For me, Angel. Please.'
Tight. Desperate.
I open my eyes. Father has turned away.
There is no bicycle, only a hospital bed.
He doesn't see me watching him.
He slumps against a wall, staring blankly at the opposite one.
I want to get out of my bed and hold him up
    the way he always had for me.
I want to wrap my arms around him tight so he can be
    happy again.
But against my will, my eyelids close
    and shut him out.

Denied

Jenna Angeline Fox.

I narrow down the possibilities.

Plus, *Accident. Boston.*

Searching for pieces with the pieces I have gained.

The Netbook blinks, and I wait for the thousands of bits to become the few I need.

A blink. Red.

Access Denied.

Denied.

Denied.

Shut out. No matter how many times I ask, it will not give it over. Why is Mr Bender allowed but I am not? What have they done to this Netbook?

Keys fly in the air. My fingers reach out. Hurry, Jenna.

The pieces speak, but there are not enough. Yet.

An Invisible Boundary

'I left the woods for as good a reason as I went there. Perhaps it seemed to me that I had several more lives to live, and could not spare any more time for that one.' Ethan pauses from his reading of *Walden* and looks in my direction.

It is the second time he has paused his reading and discussion to look at me, like he is giving me an opening to interrupt him. I don't take it, and he goes on. I am still unsure about continuing with school. It seems wrong to even be here. I am out of place. Like I am playing a game, pretending at being something I'm not. What am I? The question won't go away. Monday morning Father had to return to Boston. It was too risky to draw attention with his absence. They both said I should resume my normal routine, too. Doesn't a normal life go hand in hand with a normal routine?

I am not normal.

The group exchanges thoughts. Allys comments. Gabriel comments. Even Dane comments.

'Jenna?' Rae prompts.

I shake my head and remain silent. Rae doesn't pressure. It is not her style. She nods at Ethan to continue. He shifts his cross-legged position on the desktop and looks at me for much too long before he finally returns to the pages in his open book.

'Even though he left after two years, Thoreau decides his time at Walden is a success if only because: *I learned this, at least, by my experiment, that if one advances confidently in the direction of his dreams, and endeavors to live the life which he has imagined, he will meet with a success unexpected in common hours. He will put some things behind—*' He stops and looks at me again. I feel my agitation with him grow. His dark eyes drill into me and won't turn away, waiting. '*He will put some things behind—*' he repeats. More waiting. The silence is thunder. Dane smirks but everyone else remains quiet.

I slam my book shut and glare at him. '*He will put some things behind, will pass an invisible boundary; new, universal, and more liberal laws will begin to establish themselves around and within him; or the old laws will be expanded, and interpreted in his favor in a more liberal sense, and he will live with the license of a higher order of beings.*'

Ethan claps his hands three times. 'Thanks for joining us.'

He takes his teacher-collaborator role way too seriously. 'Thanks for forcing me,' I answer.

'So, you're good at memorization, but do you have an opinion? Is there any way to pass that invisible boundary besides dropping out like Thoreau did?'

Why is he baiting me? I feel my eyes narrow, and my voice is close to a growl when I speak. '*Nature and human life are as various as our several constitutions. Who shall say what prospect life offers to another? Could a greater miracle take place than for us to look through each other's eyes for an instant?*' Ethan's face relaxes, his eyes soften, like he has lost his mad-dog bead of concentration. But I haven't. 'Although that's just another *rote memorization,* isn't it?' I add. 'But since you might be a higher order of some sort of being, maybe if you try really hard, you can pull an opinion from it without your head exploding.'

I stand to leave. I've had enough. In Dane's words, I'm out of here. But even as I stand, I am wondering, do I look normal? What does a normal angry person look like? Should I sit back down? What am I doing? What am I? *That again.*

Another stalemate as I stand awkwardly at my desk, my hands trembling, my anger fusing with my doubts.

'Short break, Rae?' Allys suggests.

'Sure,' Rae answers, jumping on the suggestion quickly. I take it as a justified release and head for the door. Footsteps follow close behind. A trampling down the narrow hallway, past Mitch, who looks up in surprise, but we are already out the door and down the steps before she can respond.

Ethan grabs my arm from behind and swings me around. 'What's your problem?'

'What's yours? You sulk when I interrupt you, and you become an ass when I don't.'

'I don't get it. On Saturday you were kissing me like I was the last boy on the planet, and today you won't say two words to me. Not even a hello. What did your grandmother say after I left? Stay away from the dickhead?'

A lifetime has passed since I kissed him on Saturday. I am a different person now. Maybe a different *thing*. How can I explain that to him? I look at his face. I see everything. Every expression, wrinkle, twitch, doubt. More than I should. Is that the difference between a neuron and a neural chip? Can I now see deeper than the normal human perceptions? Does Father know about this? Or maybe this is normal? Was it always there for me to see, and I am only just now truly looking?

The questions may drive me mad. Even now, he wants to kiss me. I can see that, too. Would he still want to kiss if he knew about me? *Everything in the universe says it's not right.* That's *my* invisible boundary. I look at his hand, still clutching my arm, and I wonder if it will be the last time we ever touch. Should I even be thinking about these things? *Stay away.*

'Back off, loser.' Dane appears behind my shoulder.

'Stay out of this, Dane,' Ethan shoots back.

Dane pushes Ethan's shoulder. 'Go beat up someone else, lowlife.'

Ethan lets go, his eyes blinking to pinpoints, his hand held in front of him like it's on fire.

'Dane, it's not what—' Before I can finish explaining, Ethan is already gone, headed toward his truck in the parking lot.

Dane shakes his head. 'You know what he did, don't you?'

I look after Ethan. *It's better this way.* But it doesn't feel better. 'Yes,' I answer.

'I doubt it, or you'd stay away from him. He nearly killed a man. Beat him up so bad, he was in a hospital for a month.'

I think of Ethan's hand on my arm and the fear in his eyes when he let go. 'Maybe he didn't have a choice.'

'They threw him in jail for a year. I guess they thought he had a choice.'

I wonder.

'C'mon, break's over.' Dane grabs my hand and pulls me back inside.

Ethan doesn't return, and I spend the rest of the afternoon worrying about him instead of my own problems. Will he come back?

Dane tries to catch my attention over and over again. I watch him, the smile that twists his lips but never reaches his eyes. *He's missing something.* That's what Allys said. How does she know? Can she see something missing in me? He makes no secret of his flirtations. It is more of a game to him than any serious interest in me. Beat Ethan at something.

I contemplate spinning my head around three times or popping my eyeballs out and setting them on his desk. Can this freakish new body do that? The possibilities could almost amuse me. Would Dane still be so cocky then?

Probably.

The Greenhouse

Steamy droplets slide down the inside of the door. My fingers touch the glass. I am not invited in any sense.

I'm compelled to push, but why invade a space where I am not welcome?

My questions have multiplied, twisted, taken on new form. Will they ever be answered? Is ten percent enough? The most important part? Or will my questions drive me to the edge before I have the answers?

Can a thing like me even be pushed to an edge, or will I simply crash in a puff of smoke?

I gently ease open the door.

Lily is at the far end of the greenhouse. Her head turns in surprise when she sees me, but her arms are full with a large palm she is wrestling into a pot and just as quickly her attention turns back to it.

I take two more steps in. The greenhouse is at least thirty feet long. All the broken windows have now been replaced, and half the aluminum tables already hold plants. I am surprised at how warm the air inside is. Outside the sun is shining, but the February air is cool. In here, it is warm, moist, like a womb.

Lily grunts as she lifts the palm-filled pot onto the table. She turns and goes to the corner of the greenhouse where several bags are stacked, and she begins dragging one across the floor. She pauses. 'I could use some help here,' she says.

I stumble over my feet trying to reach her before she's already finished the task. She lets go of one corner of the bag as I reach for it. We both pull the bag the rest of the way and then heave it up on the table with the potted palm. She stabs into it with some shears and draws them across. Another stab and the bag is laid open and soil spills out. I don't remember this Lily, the one who is so quiet, intent, angry. The one who is so unpredictable. The pieces of Lily I remember, my nana, were not a mystery. A smile was a smile, and a sharp word was rare. Bits are still missing, but all the pieces in between are memories of her smiling every time she saw me. I wasn't just Mother and Father's North Star, but hers, too. And in many ways, I wonder if she was mine.

My teen years with her are hazy, and more often I can hear them rather than see them. *Let her be, Claire.* And then, *I think her hair is just fine.* And still later, *Give her space.* I can hear her voice lifting weights off me I didn't even know were there.

Now she is cynical, sullen, and a deeper mystery every day. She uses a small spade to transfer soil to the pot, using her bare hands to tamp it down into the sides. I stand, silent, by her side, wondering if this is all we will ever be now, both twisted versions of who we once were. The world hasn't changed. We've changed. The questions that drove me here are lost in some crippled synapse between us.

'Your mother was right, you know,' she says, interrupting my thoughts.

'What?'

'You couldn't have remembered the time you almost drowned. You were only nineteen months old. You weren't even talking yet. They say you can only remember events when you have the words to name them.'

'But I do remember, don't I?'

'Yes.'

'So maybe *they* don't know as much as they think they do.'

'No,' she says. She sets aside her spade and examines me. 'I don't suppose they do.' Our gazes rest on each other uncomfortably.

'How do I go on from here?' I blurt out. 'Do you know?'

She turns away. My question, it seems, came too fast and asked too much. 'You're the only one I can ask,' I add. 'The only one I know who will tell me the truth.'

She shakes her head. 'You've put me in such a position. Choosing between my daughter and—'

'I'll leave. I shouldn't have expected—'

'Jenna.'

The sound. My name. The sound of years ago. *Jenna.*

She spins back around. 'There are things you should know,' she says. 'Things I swore not to tell. Claire's my daughter. She means the world to me, and I would do almost anything for her'—she hesitates, drawing a deep breath—'but I think you have a right to know.'

For the first time, I am aware that I don't have a wildly beating heart—only the memory of one. But the memory is enough. My thoughts beat out of control.

She pulls two crates out from under the table and sits on one. She offers me the other. We sit knee to knee.

'I know you don't remember everything yet, but maybe I can refresh one memory. You were sixteen. You and your mother were having an argument. I had happened to stop by, but I was trying to stay out of it. She wouldn't let you go to a party. She didn't like who was giving it. The argument was going on and on, in circles, until she had finally had enough and ordered you to go to your room. Do you remember what you did?'

I shake my head.

'You laughed at her. You said you weren't seven years old and then stomped out the front door.'

'I know we had arguments but—'

'That's not my point. You *didn't go to your room.*'

I look at Lily. I don't understand the importance of rehashing an argument. So I didn't go to my room? It's over and done with. It was in the past. I can't change what happened when—

'You didn't go to your room, Jenna,' she repeats.

Okay. I didn't go—

The greenhouse spins.

Go to your room, Jenna. And I did. Compelled... even when I had a desperate need to do something else. Go to your room, Jenna. And I did.

Claire commands and it happens.

I look at Lily. My mouth opens, but I can't form any words.

'I'm sorry,' she says. 'But I'm not sorry I told you. It just isn't right.'

Control

Mother is sitting at the Netbook when I enter the kitchen. 'Good morning,' she says. 'You're up early.'

I smile. A smile that I guess must not be too different from Dane's. One that only hovers near my mouth and has no connection to anything within. 'I didn't want to miss Father when he calls,' I say cheerfully.

Lily lowers her newspaper and looks at me.

'He hasn't called yet,' Mother says, barely looking up from what she is reading. 'I'm glad you'll be able to talk to him. You went to bed so early last night. I was a little worried.'

'Because I went to my room? That's nothing to be afraid of. Do you think it is, Lily?'

'I think it's time for me to go.' She folds up her paper and stands, taking her coffee with her. 'I have things I want to get an early start on.'

'I don't blame you,' I say. 'I'd get the hell out of here, too.'

Mother looks up.

I smile and tilt my head. 'I mean, why sit around, when it's a perfectly beautiful day?'

Her brow wrinkles. 'You all right?'

'Perfect.' Another smile. 'Let me know when Father calls,' I say as I cross the kitchen. Lily is already out the door. Mother returns to her reading, and I open a kitchen cupboard and survey its contents. White plates, cups, bowls. I remove a stack of plates and set them on the island counter that is in full view of the Netbook. I lay them out one by one along the edge of the counter, rim to rim so they are like a giant pearl necklace.

The Netbook buzzes and Mother clicks Father on through. They share greetings. Father calls to me.

'Good morning, Father,' I answer.

Mother has turned and noticed the necklace of plates. I put my finger on the edge of the first plate. They both watch, confused, and before they can say anything, I press down on the lip and the plate flips and crashes to the floor.

'Jenna!' Mother says, jumping up from her chair.

'Do you have something you want to say, Mother?' I put my finger to the next plate and send it shattering to the floor as well. Father jumps in, yelling my name, and a string of other warnings that are drowned out by the third plate crashing to the floor.

'*What is the matter with you? Stop that!*' Mother yells. Father echoes similar warnings.

'Isn't there something else you want to say?' My finger is poised over the fourth plate.

I begin to bring it down, and Mother yells out, *'Go to your room, Jenna!'*

I close my eyes. I struggle. I concentrate on every twitch within me. Every joint that wants to sweep me up the stairs. I concentrate on every word I have practiced since yesterday.

Don't go, Jenna.

Don't go.

Don't go.

I open my eyes. I remain in place. I have not gone anywhere. I am drained from the effort.

I glare at them both. 'How dare you!' I say. 'How dare you play with my brain! How dare you pretend with me that I'm normal! How dare you program me!'

The word sends a shockwave through the room. For a moment neither one speaks, stunned by the outing of their dirty secret.

'Jenna, come here,' Father finally says. 'Come closer to the screen. Sit, so we can talk.'

'Do I have a choice? Or is that another thing that is programmed into me. *Sit down, Jenna. Sit down! Sit down!'*

'Jenna, please,' Mother pleads.

'Jenna Angeline Fox!' Father says. 'Look at you. Are you in your room right now? No. You're obviously not programmed. Let me explain!' I don't move. 'Angel,' he adds.

I step forward and sit in the kitchen chair Mother has pulled up to the Netbook. Am I doing this of my own free will? I'm not sure.

'It was a suggestion, Jenna. We only planted a strong suggestion. Like a subliminal message. It wasn't programming. And it was for your own protection. You've been through a terrible trauma, not unlike any patient who has had a severe brain injury. Erratic behavior can sometimes be a side effect of such an injury. Usually medication is used to lessen adverse effects. But medicine won't work with you, Jenna. You don't have the same circulatory system or nervous system of other brain-injury patients. So a very simple thing we did was plant something that is no more controlling than a subliminal message in case you started behaving out of control.'

Who is really out of control here?

'I don't want you to control me,' I say.

'We don't,' Mother says firmly. 'Like your father said, you're here and not in your room. Right? But until you could understand everything that has happened, we also had to have a way to get you out of sight fast if we had to. For your own protection, and others', too. We've already told you that a lot of people have put their lives and careers on the line for you. If someone should show up here unexpectedly, someone asking questions—'

'We've taken a lot of precautions, Jenna,' Father interrupts. 'But if someone were to see you right now, it would be difficult to explain. Your organ failures, severe burns, limb losses—it was all on hospital records. We've managed to make changes to a lot of those records, and we're still trying to make more. But we can't change what people saw. There are a lot of medical staff who would remember. A lot who knew you were beyond the limits of what the FSEB legally allows. For now, the official story we've given everyone is that you're stabilized and receiving private nursing care at an undisclosed location. That alone has been a source of questions and rumor because no one expected you to live, much less recover. If they were to see you as you are now, it would certainly lead to an investigation, or worse. Let's face it, I'm news, and with my background with Bio Gel and the high profile of Fox BioSystems, red flags would go flying. The media would have a field day and the FSEB would be out to make an example of us. Everyone involved would be facing jail time. And I'm not sure what would happen—'

He doesn't finish. He doesn't need to. I can fill in the unspeakable blank. Me. What would they do to the uploaded thing that is me?

'That's why we didn't want you to go to school, but we knew that eventually we had to let you have your life back, too, or what would be the point of it all? But no one knows where you and your mother are. The house was bought under Lily's name, and I keep my travels there to a bare minimum to avoid anyone tracking us down.

'And as I said,' he continues, 'we've been making adjustments to hospital records and eventually as time passes, if someone sees you and questions anything, we can attribute discrepancies to faulty memories. So it was for your protection, too. Since you didn't understand the whole scope of what is going on, we had to have a way to remove you from a potentially harmful situation. You have to see that we felt we had to plant this suggestion.'

'And just how did you "plant" this suggestion?' I ask.

Father opens his mouth to answer, but Mother intervenes. 'It was uploaded,' she says plainly.

I close my eyes. This or the dark place? It is a draw. I open my eyes and look first at Mother, then at Father. 'Is there anything else you thought it *necessary* to upload? We may as well get it all out right now.'

There is a prolonged pause, each waiting to see how forthcoming the other is. My question is answered. There is something else.

I sigh and lean back in the chair.

'You were missing so much school,' Mother says. 'You were so sick. We knew you would have enough challenges as it was, and we honestly didn't think you'd ever be able to go to school again.'

'It was a mistake. We realize that now,' Father says. 'But we uploaded the tenth-through-twelfth-grade curriculum of the Boston Unified School District. It was probably too much information—not what you would have absorbed naturally—but we can't take it back. It doesn't work that way. Not without starting from scratch.'

None of it is really mine.

My synapses fire like a fireworks display.

Thoreau.

The French Revolution.

The earthquake, the Second Great Depression, current events. Word by word.

The invisible boundary.

Ten percent.

The most important part.

Who shall say what prospect life offers to another?

To live deep and suck out all the marrow.

All of it.

I look at my hands. Clasp them and unclasp them. Perfect. Monster. Hands.

A thousand points. A thousand illegal points.

Clasping. Unclasping.

The butterfly.

Suck out the marrow.

The marrow of Jenna Fox.

My feet fidget. They tap. The way they always did. The nervous gesture of my childhood. My borrowed feet remember. Something that is still mine. I calm them.

'Then I should have the key to the closet,' I finally say.

Mother looks at Father. She is not the deferring type. But in all these uncertain matters she defers to him. I see this is not her world. She is feeling her way through something foreign. She only wanted her daughter back. Would pay any price for it. But the price is navigating uncertainty and secrets that seem to keep spinning faster than she is. She's wide-eyed, staring at the Netbook and Father. He remains steady, his eyes faltering for only a microsecond. But it's a faltering microsecond that is a lifetime for me. I can see. He is afraid. Maybe terrified. He calculates his reply. 'What do you mean, Jenna?' he asks calmly.

What are they afraid of? What do they think—

I feel a ping, chilling and alert. *The key.*

Their eyes are riveted on me, invested, waiting for an answer. 'The key to the small door at the back of my closet,' I tell them. I see the visible relief on both their faces. 'If I need to really get out of sight one day, it would be logical to go there.'

'Yes, of course,' Father agrees.

'I have it somewhere. I'll find it,' Mother says. She is too eager. She rummages through a drawer and produces two keys. 'I think it's one of these.'

'I'll go try them both.'

I hurry upstairs to my closet, pocketing the keys Mother handed me. I rush, afraid she may follow. I overturn my hamper and riffle through dirty clothes and sheets, looking for the pants I wore four days ago. I find them and search the pocket. The key to Mother's closet is still there. This is the key that made Father falter, the one he thought I was talking about.

I scan my closet for a hiding place. I kneel in the corner and pull back the carpet, tuck the key there, and carefully push the carpet back down on the tack strip. I place my hand over the patch of carpeting, like some truth will filter through. Something that is all, one hundred percent, mine.

My hand hovers, but no truth comes, only the knowledge that maybe this is my way of balancing the power.

Trust

It's midnight. The house is dark. Quiet. Mother and Lily have been in bed for an hour.

I watch Year Seven/Jenna Fox. It's the only disc I have watched more than once. This is my fourth time.

Seven-year-old Jenna leads Father through the house. He has a blindfold on. Lily must be filming. Glimpses of Mother smiling and following along, giggles from Jenna, and hollow protests from Father punctuate the journey.

'Where are you taking me, Jenna?'

'You can't ask, Daddy!' Jenna wails.

'The moon?'

'Daddy!'

'The *Mayflower*?'

I watch Father being pulled, pushed, and turned. He trusts me as I lead him from room to room and down hallways. Step up.

Step down. He exaggerates his movements, lifting his feet like he is stepping onto a stage. But he trusts me. He trusts seven-year-old Jenna. What did I do to make that change?

They reach the kitchen doorway. A large, lopsided blue cake is on the kitchen table, candles already burned halfway down during the long, blindfolded walk. The icing sags and bunches out on one side like a slow-moving glacier, bringing tipping candles along with it.

'Stop!' Jenna says. 'Turn. No, this way, Daddy! Bend down. Ready?'

I remove the blindfold. 'Surprise!' Mother and I yell and clap our hands. Father throws his hands in the air. He gasps. Jenna beams. Her gap-toothed smile is nearly angelic.

'It's beautiful! It's perfect! It's the best cake I've ever had!'

'She made it herself,' Mother says proudly. 'We doubled the batch because she wanted it big.'

Mother and Father share a glance, a brief look that flies over Jenna's bouncing head. It is a full look just between them. A look of love, satisfaction, fulfillment. Easiness. Completeness. Everything they want and need is right in that room.

'It's big, all right! And *blue*!' He continues to praise and adore it. Just as he adores Jenna.

I watch them dig in with forks and no plates. More laughter. More squeals. More looks.

It makes me feel all the ways I've wanted to feel ever since I woke up.

Trusted.

Happy.

Enough.

Father takes a fingerful of blue icing and decorates Jenna's nose, and she squeals.

And now, in the quiet of my room, I laugh, too. I laugh out loud.

Just as I have done every time I've watched it.

Sanctuary

The church is empty. No priests. No Lily. Not even sweet singing voices to stir the air. The sanctuary is in the shape of a cross. I stand in the crosshairs, feeling like an imposter, waiting to be found at any moment and ushered out.

Sanctuary.

I weigh the meanings. A holy place. Refuge.

A place of forgiveness.

Rows of candles flicker on either side of me in the smaller arms of the church. I step forward, my clumsy feet scuffing the floor, echoing across the stillness. Souls, if there is such a thing, are nourished and mended here. In case of error they can't be uploaded like the whole Boston curriculum—there are no spares in case one is lost. Souls are given only once.

I walk up the three steps to the altar and step over the small railing that separates the masses from all that is sacred. I am trespassing, but I can't stop. I wait to feel something. Something different. But who knows what a soul feels like?

I dare to step closer, violating the holy space that surrounds me. I rest my hands on the altar, feeling the linen cloth only meant for a priest's fingers. History. I can feel it in the threads. I close my eyes, searching for my own history, the intangible bits that will tell me if what I am is enough.

A voice booms. 'You shouldn't be up there.'

My eyes fly open and I turn around. Just as quickly, I turn back, carefully placing my hands on the altar, willing them not to tremble. I ignore the warning and the footsteps getting closer.

'Still can't talk to the dickhead, hm?'

Oh, God. I have to say something. 'That's not a word you should be using in church,' I answer.

I hear him getting closer, his footsteps softening as he walks up the steps. 'Then I guess we both have one mark against us. You walking where you shouldn't, and me saying a bad word.'

I hear a few more steps and his shoe banging the railing as he steps over it. I turn around and face him. 'Two.'

'What?'

'I only have one mark against me. You have two. You also stepped over the railing.'

His face contorts to an unflattering mix of frustration and anger. '*You are so*—' but just as quickly, his scowl is gone and the sharpness vanishes. His soft brown eyes stare into mine for a second or two. Or three. 'Jenna,' he sighs, 'I don't want to argue. I just came looking for you. You were supposed to meet me over an hour ago down at the lavanderia. If you don't want to work on the project with me anymore, Father Rico has someone else who—'

'No,' I say.

He walks closer, an arm's length from me. 'No, you don't want to work with me?'

I can't answer. What I should say and what I want to say are two different things. Have I always been this mixed up?

Ethan grabs my arms. 'Jenna, you have to talk to me.'

'I need to—I want to keep working with you, Ethan. But—'

He bends over and kisses me.

And I kiss him back.

We are kissing on the altar. We are passionately kissing on the altar of the church in front of all the sainted statues. How many marks against us is that?

I push him away. 'This isn't right,' I say.

'Listen, I know I've done some things in the past—'

'Ethan. This isn't about you. Things have changed. It's me. There are things.'

'Tell me,' he says.

I look into his eyes. They call them windows to the soul. I think I can see Ethan's. What does he see when he looks into mine? I look away and see more eyes, the statues of the saints watching us from their niches. Joseph. Mary. Saint Francis. Their gazes split me wide.

You mustn't tell.

For all our sakes.

Especially yours.

You mustn't say anything to anyone.

'Not here,' I tell him. 'Let's go outside.'

Telling

Like the church, the cemetery is empty, but here there are no corners or shadows to hide listening ears. Just the dead. They may hear, but they can't tell and never will. They are one step past the dark place. I haven't even told my parents about that. How can I tell Ethan?

We walk on the grass, stepping over and around the tarnished markers that remember lives and moments in time. Where we are going, I don't know. It doesn't seem to be the place that is important but the steps in between. Ethan finally stops at a dark, moldy niche holding a statue of a watchful saint that is streaked with years of weather and grime. This must be the place of telling.

My head hurts. It's the first time I have felt this kind of pain. Almost like a headache. Are my biochips punishing me for trying to reveal the truth? Maybe I am programmed never to admit anything? Maybe I am self-destructing even as I stand here. I wince and drop my head into my hands, rubbing my temples.

'Never mind, Jenna. You don't have to tell me,' Ethan says.

I press my temples, trying to sort it out. 'I need to,' I say. 'I have to tell someone.'

It is odd. The sun is shining. The grass is a brilliant green. The cemetery is almost festive, with colorful flowers dotting the neatly trimmed graves. It is a shocking contrast to the ugly truth I am about to reveal to Ethan.

I lay my hands out, palms up, toward him. 'Take my hands,' I say. He does. He squeezes them. I wonder at the feelings it sends up my arms, through my brain, through all that is salvaged and new. I wonder at what is real and what is replicated, the braiding of genuine and fake. I wonder at the miracle Father has fashioned. 'It's not real, Ethan,' I tell him. His brows draw together and he shakes his head. 'The accident,' I tell him. 'I lost my hands in the accident. These are created. Like prosthetics.'

He gently turns my hands and examines them, as though he doesn't believe me. 'They're beautiful,' he says. He doesn't let go. He caresses them. 'Can you feel this?'

I nod. I feel every callus and crease of his fingers. I feel touch in ways I never did before. Velvety, fluid, and when I concentrate, I can almost feel his skin as my own. I sigh. 'This isn't all, Ethan. There's more.'

'Like?'

'My arms. My legs.' I watch his eyes. I look for the slightest bit of revulsion, but none is there. Yet. 'Nearly everything,' I blurt out. His eyes are steady. 'Enough that I'm illegal. *Very* illegal. According to the point schedule Allys told me about, I could be illegal five times over.' His eyes falter and I feel everything in me cave. I pull my hands loose. 'So that's why my grandmother doesn't want me to see you. She is trying to spare you, not me. By her own words, she doesn't know what to make of me. Neither do I, except that I'm some kind of freakish monster.'

Ethan walks away. He comes back, his hands jammed into his pockets. He stares at me. His face is stiff. Frightening. I feel weak. What have I done? I should have kept quiet. Listened to Mother. To Lily. I want to take back every word, but it is too late.

His soft brown eyes have turned to icy beads. All his warmth is gone. 'I nearly killed a man, Jenna,' he says. 'Some people called me a monster for hitting him with a bat even after he was unconscious. But I never felt like a monster. I barely remember doing it—something inside me snapped.' Sweat spreads across his face, even though the day is cool. His confession runs out in choppy breaths, on the heels of mine, like they are linked.

'The guy was a dealer. He gave my brother HCP. My brother was only thirteen at the time, Jenna. He didn't know anything about anything. So I went after the dealer. When they sentenced me, they said they couldn't tolerate people out there like me, trying to wield their own form of law enforcement. "Vigilante justice", they called it. It wasn't justice. This guy's free and my brother's hooked. He's been in and out of rehab ever since.'

He pauses and draws in a long, shaky breath. 'So I know what a monster is, Jenna, and it's not me, and it's not you.' His voice is choked. It is like my fear exposed his own. I slide my arms around his back and hold him, strumming the knots of his spine and the blade of his shoulder, weighing the events that have made us both who we are now. His lips nestle close to my ear, and I feel his labored breaths on my skin. 'Don't tell Allys,' he finally whispers.

'About you?'

He holds me tighter. 'No. About you.'

Would They Ask That of Someone Who Was Real?

There were no days.

There were no nights.

Eighteen months was nothing.

And it was eternity.

Sixteen years of thought trapped in circuitry.

A spinning glass ball.

Shattering inward, moment by airless moment.

But everyone says, *Don't tell.*

How can I not?

A Science Lesson

'Catch up, Dane!' I hear the bite in Rae's voice. Her seemingly endless smile and patience must have its own invisible boundary. Dane flashes a smile from the top of the ravine and nods, but his face goes instantly expressionless when she turns away. I've heard about sociopaths, people who connect with no one but themselves and their own self-interests. That would be Dane.

I walk next to Allys as we make our way to a creek bed for our outdoor science and ethics session. Allys chose the site, which surprises me. She walks down the incline without her braces.

'You're doing better,' I say.

'Yes, the new software was a match. Right on target. They said it would take a few weeks, and here it is three weeks later. It's reduced the phantom pains, too.'

'That's wonderful.'

She shrugs. 'Not the real thing, though. It never will be. It's a patch, that's all.'

'You're bitter?'

She stops to rest and smiles at me. I think of the time she told me, *I like you, Jenna.* Her face is soft like that right now. 'Do I seem bitter?' she asks. 'I hope not. Not that there aren't days. But I'm trying to channel that bitterness into determination. Maybe I can make a difference for someone else. That's all.'

'By volunteering in the ethics office?'

'Yes, I guess so. I want to make sure science is held accountable in the future so others won't have to go through what I've been through. But I'm grateful for these.' She gestures with her prosthetics. 'Truly I am. They aren't perfect, but none of us are ever exactly what we want to be, right?'

'Right,' I answer.

'When I *was* going through my bitter phase, my counselor told me we're all products of our parents, genes, or environment in one way or another.' She begins walking again. 'And I may wish I could change the hand I was dealt, but I can't, so all I can do now is choose how I will play it. So that's what I'm doing. Playing it the best I can.'

'Dane!' Rae calls.

An unenthusiastic 'Coming' is heard from above.

'Speaking of genes and a bad hand,' Allys says, glancing over her shoulder and rolling her eyes.

I stop and grab her arm, jerking her to a halt. 'I like you, Allys.'

She looks at me, a wrinkle running across her forehead. 'I like you, too, Jenna,' she says slowly. Ethan is already below, sitting on a rock by the creek. I can see his warning look.

I look back at Allys. 'I just wanted to tell you,' I say. 'It's important that you know.'

'Sure,' she answers. She tags on an awkward smile.

I am an oaf. My timing is off. But I had to get it out. Some things you have to tell, no matter how stupid they may sound. Some things you can't save for later. There might not be a later.

We arrive at the creek and the scattering of boulders that will be our classroom. Rae is there for support, but Allys is teacher-collaborator for this session. Dane finally arrives and sits on a nearby swooping oak branch rather than join the covey of boulders we sit on. Rae wears hiking boots and blue jeans. They fit her better than the suits she usually wears. I look at my own clothes, the simple shirts and slacks provided by Claire. Light blue, dark blue. They have the personality of a slug.

'You can hear from there, Dane?' Rae asks.

'Perfectly,' he answers, then adds his trademark soulless smile.

Allys begins her discussion with some review of the manipulation of the Bt bacterium to create pest-resistant crops, and the introduction of transgenic animals into the food supply decades ago. 'Of course, at the time, all of these "breakthroughs" seemed like a good thing, especially from an economic standpoint—'

'We had to hike all the way down here to hear this?' Dane groans.

'What's the matter? Had to break a sweat?' Gabriel shoots back. I am surprised. Gabriel avoids confrontation. Maybe, like Rae, he has a boundary, too, and it's been crossed too many times. Dane stares at Gabriel but doesn't respond, no expression on his mouth or in his eyes. A dead look. It is more disturbing than a glare. It is impossible to know what he is thinking.

'I know you have the patience of a rapidly decomposing turd, Dane, but I will get to my reason for meeting here. Not that I need one. Sunshine is plenty for most people.' Allys adjusts her position on her rock, unaware of how much satisfaction she has brought to Ethan and Gabriel. Maybe even Rae.

'Before the FSEB stepped in to regulate science labs, bioengineered plants and transgenic animals were being introduced into the food chain at the rate of dozens of species a year. Since these posed no direct health concern to humans, the FDA was approving these introductions at an alarming pace. But—'

I know where she is going. I shouldn't interrupt, but my

167

mouth is speaking before I can decide not to. 'But no one looked at the effects of these new species intermingling with native populations? That's the danger, isn't it?'

'Exactly,' she answers. 'They didn't even consider the possibility. That's why regulation is key.'

'To make sure we don't produce any lab monsters?' I offer. 'Ones that might get out in the world and taint the original species? Is that what you mean?' Ethan stands and leaps to an adjacent rock to get my attention. He wants me to shut up. Do Allys and my secret frighten him that much?

'Well, Jenna,' she answers, 'I'm not sure *taint* is quite the right word. It's more like making sure native populations aren't put at risk. It's already too late for so many species, which is why the work of the Federal Science Ethics Board is so—'

Ethan leaps to another rock, his hands flying over his head at the same time. 'But that's the sticking point, isn't it, Allys? Even the FSEB has its share of scandal. Payoffs. Conflict of interests. Sleeping with—'

'Ethan! What federal agency doesn't have its problems? All the things you're mentioning were early in its history.'

Rae watches intently. She seems gratified that a simple science lesson has turned unexpectedly passionate.

'Besides,' Allys continues, 'those issues have been worked out. And now, without their careful monitoring, who knows what labs would be unleashing on the world?'

I stand. 'Probably a lot of illegal things,' I say. 'Freakish things.' I walk toward Allys. 'Dangerous things.' The freakish me, my delivery, my timing, everything about me, off. Different. Unleashed.

'Right,' Allys says. She stares at me. Quiet. Wondering at my opinion? Or my awkward stance? Or the fact that I am only an arm's length away, meeting her stare. Her mind is racing. *What is wrong with Jenna Fox? Something is different.* She senses it. I can see it in every eyelash, every contraction of her pupil. She is searching. Trying to fill the gaps between her own synapses. Am I really that different from her?

Time is suspended. I can feel the breath of Ethan, Rae, and Gabriel, held between us.

'Why are we here?' Dane's voice cuts through.

Allys turns to face Dane. She spits her words out at him. 'A short *forty* years ago, you hopeless moron, you would have been underwater. Look at the top of this ravine! This was once a river. In just forty short years, thanks to transgenic intervention and its domino effects, this tributary has become a mostly dry creek bed. So that is why we're here, *Dane.* End of lesson!'

I look at the sparse trickle. I look at the dry boulders. I look at what science has done.

To me. To the ravine. And finally, to Allys.

Yes.

End of lesson.

Red

My fingers brush along the hangers in my closet. First my shirts, then my pants, all varying shades of blue. Sturdy. Neat. Functional. None with a fraction of the flair that I saw in Rae's clothes. These have no personality at all.

Even Gabriel, who wants to fade into the background more than any of us, looks like a strutting peacock compared to me. Yesterday, when we climbed back out of the ravine, Dane and Gabriel were the last ones out. No one saw what happened. Dane claimed he lost his footing, but it was Gabriel who went down. His shirt was nearly ripped off his back. Back in the car, Gabriel fumed. He knew it wasn't an accident, but all he said was, 'This was my favorite shirt.' *My favorite shirt.* It struck me then. I don't have a favorite shirt. And now suddenly it seems so very important.

I pull out two shirts and compare them. There is no reason to like one more than the other. They almost look like lab attire. The only thing I like is—

The color.

A memory catches me.

Kara and I are shopping on Newbury Street, running in and out of tiny shops on a rainy spring day. We finally hunker down in our favorite. Kara chides me: *Jenna, I refuse to allow you to buy another blue skirt! Your whole closet is blue!*

My favorite color was blue.

And Kara's favorite color was red.

Claire may have had to choose my clothes hastily, or maybe she chose them because they wouldn't draw attention, but at least she tried to get a color she knew I liked. But that day almost two years ago, Kara talked me into the red skirt. She was right. It was a change I needed. What happened to that red skirt? Couldn't Mother have packed my clothes and brought them from Boston? Or maybe that was part of the secret. A gravely ill, bedridden Jenna would have no use for short red skirts or floppy flowered hats, or jewel-trimmed blouses, and that invalid picture had to be preserved for prying eyes. Besides, a new, improved, and shorter Jenna would need new pants anyway. Ones that wouldn't drag and reveal her lost two inches.

I ache for that red skirt now.

And I ache for the day I bought it with Kara.

Sliver

The lane to Mr Bender's house is quiet. A breeze rustles golden leaves end over end along the gutter. The same breeze cuts across my face. It is cold, but I don't shiver. It's only California cold, not Boston cold. Mother and Father claim I will never feel that cold again.

Maybe.

Do I really want to live for two hundred years? Then again, do I want to live for only two either? Is that decision up to me? I am nearly eighteen. Eighteen what? An eighteen-year-old thing that can make a choice? If Father really believes what he says, that there is a most important ten percent, then one day I may make the choice to go to Boston. Kara and Locke are in Boston.

A gust whips my hair across my face, and I startle, stopping in the street, closing my eyes but still seeing, remembering the feeling, brushing strands from my face two years ago, the saltiness, the crispness, the foamy spray of a nearby crashing wave, the sound of gulls overhead, the feeling of sand between my toes.

These memories descend out of nowhere, giving me pieces of who I was, but their significance is lost. I sigh and resume my walk, not knowing if this memory is important, or just more of the jumbled trivia of Jenna's life, like sock shopping. Maybe that is all any life is composed of, trivia that eventually adds up to a person, and maybe I just don't have enough of it yet to be a whole one.

My half-filled memory is pocked with extremes: flashes of surgical clarity paired with syrupy-slow searches for basic words any four-year-old would know, moments of startling insights followed by fits of embarrassing denseness, vast gaps where I can't even remember what happened to my best friends, and then glimpses from my infancy that should never be remembered. But then when I am feeling the least human, I remember kissing Ethan and feeling intensely alive—more alive than I think the old Jenna could have ever felt. Would that make a difference to the FSEB?

In dark, silent moments in the middle of the night, alone, I count the number of times my chest rises, watching with detached interest this thing that I am, knowing my breaths don't take in oxygen—it is only for show. I am almost impressed with the rhythm of it all, in a repulsive sort of way. And then it leads me, unexpectedly, back to a place where I can almost feel my fingers touching who I used to be. Jenna. The real Jenna.

I wonder. Is there such a thing? A real Jenna? Or was the old me always waiting to be someone else, too?

Hurry, Jenna. Hurry. Kara's and Locke's voices won't let go.

Or maybe it's me who won't let go.

I jiggle the latch on Mr Bender's gate and swing it open. His house reminds me of Thoreau's Walden. It is larger, but still rustic and natural, overgrown with landscape, banks of wild white roses tangling across the porch roof. He doesn't answer when I knock.

I walk around to the side and down his long driveway. I see him examining a window on his garage.

'Hello,' I call.

He turns and waves. 'Good to see you.'

I walk closer and see the window is shattered.

'You broke it?'

'Someone did.' He says *someone* like it's a name.

I look inside. Tables are overturned. Paint is thrown against walls. An upholstered stool is slashed and the stuffing pulled out and tossed. But it is the aqua-colored car parked within that stops me. The dusty cover has been partially ripped away to reveal an old and obviously out-of-commission car. *I've seen that car before.* But I don't know where. Maybe in a photo? Or maybe I've only seen one just like it.

'Did you call the police?' I ask.

'No. I don't want to get them involved.'

'Because of your secret?'

'I have to weigh the risks. This isn't worth it. I can clean this up in a few hours, and the monetary loss isn't more than a few hundred dollars. What bothers me most is they didn't take anything—at least as far as I can tell. I have tools worth thousands of dollars in there. They didn't want that. Just the sick pleasure of destroying something that belongs to someone else.' Like the first day I met him, he looks off in the distance toward the white house at the end of my street, and he shakes his head.

'I can help you clean it up,' I say.

'Not now. I need a cup of tea. I'll do it later.'

'May I ask a favor, then? Can I use your Netbook?'

He hesitates.

'Mine's broken,' I add. It is only a small lie.

'Let's go.'

With a few carefully worded inquiries, the facts spit forth freely. Mother and Father would be horrified. I am equally horrified, knowing that this is another suspicion confirmed—they are still keeping secrets from me. Important ones. Are there others? Nothing is denied by Mr Bender's Netbook as it was with mine. He brews a cup of tea and gives me privacy as he shuffles through some proofs. News clip after news clip fills in holes and at the same time creates new ones. They wrap around me in ways I hadn't considered. I feel...what? Mother's breathlessness? The need to look away? My bioengineered blood pooling at my feet?

I lean back and stare at the screen. 'You knew about Kara and Locke, didn't you?'

Mr Bender sets aside his proofs and nods.

I stare at the screen, absorbing word by word a sliver of my life that changed everything.

> *In spite of a pending civil action, the district attorney's office reports that it has no plans at this time to prosecute Jenna Fox, 16, daughter of Matthew Fox, founder of Fox BioSystems, based here in Boston. There were no apparent witnesses to the accident. Passenger Locke Jenkins, also 16, died two weeks after the accident without regaining consciousness. Kara Manning, 17, the second passenger, sustained severe head trauma when she was thrown from the car and as a result could not give investigators any information. She died three weeks following the accident when her family removed life support.*

My fingers shake. I press the key to bring up the next page.

> *Fox, who didn't yet have a driver's license, is semicomatose and still in critical condition. The severity of her burns and injuries makes it impossible for her to communicate or give authorities any details about the accident. Investigators say they can't rule out the possible involvement of a second car, but it appears that high speeds and reckless driving contributed to the car veering off Route 93 and tumbling 140 feet down the steep incline. The hydrogen in the tri-energy BMW, registered to Matthew Fox, exploded on impact, leaving investigators little evidence to piece together events from the evening of the crash.*

I close Mr Bender's Netbook.

Somehow I knew I would never see them again.

Something deep inside me told me they were dead.

How? When? Before they scanned my brain, before they removed my ten percent, did I hear someone at the hospital talking? Did Mother sob for Locke, then Kara, at my bedside, knowing her daughter was responsible for it all?

But I wasn't.

I couldn't have been responsible.

'It's not true,' I say. 'I didn't do that. I would remember.'

'You lost two friends. You may have blocked it out.'

Or someone did.

No wonder Mother and Father won't talk about it. I killed my best friends. *High speeds and reckless driving.* Their precious Jenna wasn't so perfect after all.

Hurry, Jenna. Is that why the words keep circling through me?

Trying to remind me of what I did? Strangely, I feel something, but it is not guilt. Does that make me a monster?

I remember. Something. A bit.

A black sky. Stars. The halo of a streetlight.

Here. Throw them. Keys flying through the air. My hand stretched out. *Hurry, Jenna.* A glimpse of the night everything changed. Mother and Father may have blocked out most of it, but they couldn't get rid of it all. A tattletale neurochip decided I would get a hooded peek of what I had done. Is the joke on Father, or me?

Mr Bender suggests a walk in the garden. He feeds the birds and they peck in his palm. I stretch out my palm briefly, but again they don't come to me. And maybe now I know why.

One Simple Thing

I rip open boxes. Box after box. Books. Dishes. Papers. Clothing. Keepsakes. I dump them out. Box. After box. After box. I ransack. I search. I break.

None of it is mine.

I collapse in the midst of the disaster I have created in the garage, and garbled noises crawl up my throat.

It sounds like an animal.

I am.

I am a kept animal.

With no past but what they will give me.

And all I wanted today was one simple thing.

A red skirt.

Another Dark Place

'Floor to ceiling, don't you think?' Claire points her laser to the ceiling and records the measurement.

'Fine,' I say. I watch her, measuring for drapes for my window. I take in the angles of the room, the slant of light flooding through panes of glass, the planes that separate us, the irony of drapes to create darkness.

I stare at her. My mother is an older version of me, but she is also something I will never be. Old. My skin and bones will not age—my Bio Gel will simply reach the end of its shelf life and cease to operate. If I were to marry, I would not grow old with my husband. I could either die after two years or outlive him by a hundred. An interesting prospect. What price did Claire pay to keep her only child?

She sees me staring, and it makes her busier. She chatters, fills space, is careful but does not address my gaze. She treads even faster to keep on the surface, but somehow I don't count it against her. She said that for months she was in as dark a place as I. Maybe staying on the surface keeps her from returning to a place where she can't breathe. She measures length and depth as carefully as a surgeon places a scalpel, as though it is a matter of life and death. Maybe for her it is.

She is always careful around me. Is that why the word hovers close in my thoughts? Careful with her movements, careful with her words. Nothing is relaxed between us. Is she careful because she thinks I will break? Or maybe because she will. When I am alone in the dark counting my breaths, is she doing the same in the darkness of her room, wondering . . . was it all worth it?

Now, with light streaming through the window, she is busy, determined to gain control over what is natural. Each of her movements is like a blow, a punch, a fist kneading something into shape.

'Accident,' I say.

Her laser clicks off. She looks at me, instantly pale, her eyes sunken. 'What?'

'I've learned how to say it. *Accident.* I assume that was another suggestion you and Father planted, to never bring up the accident.'

She sets her laser down on my nightstand. She looks at me blankly. Weak.

'No,' she says, easing herself down to the edge of my bed, 'I think it was something inside of you not allowing you to say it.' She nods her head, like she is plucking together words she has been saving. 'And we didn't want to push you.'

'They're dead,' I say.

Her eyes glisten. She holds her arms out to me, and I slip through space like a feather on a current of wind, effortlessly carried by the force that is Claire.

I sit on the bed next to her, feeling her arms holding me, rocking us together in primal rhythm. 'We tried to bring it up at the hospital,' she whispers, her breath and tears warm on my cheek. 'It was too hard for you. You went into distress just trying to communicate. Shortly after, you slipped into a coma. We were afraid that we had made it worse, pushing you too hard. We didn't want to make that mistake again.' She pulls away and looks into my eyes. 'It was an accident, Jenna. An *accident.* You don't have to relive the details.'

'Is that why you blocked it all from our Netbook?'

She nods again. 'When you woke up, you didn't seem to remember it. We didn't want you to come upon something unexpectedly and have a setback.'

She pulls me close again, my head on her chest. I can hear her heartbeat. Familiar. The sound I heard in her womb. The whoosh, the beat, the flow that punctuated my beginnings in another dark place. I had no words for those sounds then, just feelings. Now I have both. I can remember it as clearly as I remember yesterday.

We lie back on my pillows, holding each other without talking, and time becomes a forgotten detail. Seconds and minutes stretch into an hour or more. I don't want to move. Claire strokes my forehead, dozing, the slant of light through my panes growing golden, then dim, the afternoon passing.

'I'm sorry,' I finally whisper. Sorry for Locke and Kara. Sorry for her months of worry. Sorry for how we have to live now. Sorry for pushing her away. Sorry that I'm not perfect.

'Shhh,' she says, stroking my head again. And then she adds, 'I'm sorry, too.'

I see the ring of swatches, sitting on my nightstand. 'The swatches,' I say, 'they're all blue. Do you have any that are red?'

'Red?'

'Can I have red drapes?'

'You can have anything you want. Anything.'

I close my eyes, pressing my ear to her chest again. Hearing the sounds, the pulse of Claire, the world of my beginnings, the time when there was no doubt I had a soul. When I existed in a warm, velvet liquid that was as dark as night, and that dark place was the only place I wanted to be.

Percentages

I fold a yellowed lace tablecloth and lay it in the bottom of a box. 'I'm sorry about the vase. I—I wasn't careful.'

Lily makes a sound. I am not sure if it is a snort or a laugh. 'That's an understatement.'

I heard her cursing this morning. I knew immediately why and ran out the back door. She had discovered my rampage in the garage when she raised the door to take the car out.

'I don't have any money, but I'll find a way to replace it.'

She doesn't address my offer. 'Breaking things seems to be your new specialty. I almost wish I hadn't left the morning you started flipping plates for your parents.'

'It wasn't amusing.'

'Not at the time, I'm sure.'

I close a filled box and begin filling another. Everything in here belongs to Lily. 'Why are your things out here in boxes?'

'They were supposed to go to storage. Before I came here, I was—well—I suppose you could say that I was getting out of Dodge.'

'Dodge?'

'It's an old saying. It means getting out of town before there's trouble. Except that I was getting out of the country. I knew you were—that your parents would be—' She sighs and shakes dirt from a cashmere fedora. 'I knew that it was about time.'

Time. Almost like a rebirth. 'What was it like?'

Lily startles. 'What do you mean?'

'Did you see the construction?' It sounds harsh. It is. It *was.*

She vigorously shakes her head. 'Oh, no. Once I knew what they were up to, I stayed at my place in Kennebunk. Your mother and I hardly talked during that period.'

'You didn't approve.'

She is quiet, laying the fedora in the top of a full box and closing it. She pulls two feet of tape from the roll, the screech cutting through the dusty silence. '*Approve* is probably not the right word,' she finally says. '*Shock,* maybe. Or *fear.*' She thinks for a moment longer and adds, 'Maybe *approve* is the right word. I don't know. It was the unknown.'

I understand. It's the unknown that I fear—the bits of memories that still have no connections; the role I played in Kara's and Locke's deaths; the voices that linger, too fresh; the constant game of weighing percentages, wondering if ten percent of one thing can be worth as much as ninety percent of something else. And then the answer that always runs through my neurons and neurochips: unknown.

'That's one thing Mother and Father didn't plan on—the unknown. There's a lot I haven't told them.'

She perks up, looking almost pleased that I have found fault with Mother and Father's little coup. 'Like what?' she asks.

'Remembering my baptism, and even earlier memories.'

'Are you sure?'

I nod. 'It frightened me at first, but now, somehow it comforts me. Like I have every bit of who I was, maybe even more than the Jenna I used to be ever had. Maybe it makes up for what I've lost. Maybe it balances the percentages?'

'Percentages!' she huffs. 'Those are for economists, polls, and politicians. Percentages can't define your identity.' She stacks books in a box and looks up. 'What else haven't you told them?'

I am still mulling over the word *identity* as I answer her. 'I hear voices.'

'You mean memories?'

I hesitate. 'I'm not sure,' I tell her. 'Sometimes they seem too...fresh. Like they're whispering right into my ear.'

She stiffens. 'Who?' she asks.

'Kara and Locke. At least I think it's them.'

She sits on a nearby box.

'I know about them,' I say. 'I know they're dead.'

'You remember the accident.'

'No. I read about it. But I think I already knew, somewhere inside. It didn't shock me when I found out. It was more like a confirmation.'

She looks up at the rafters, the air, her gaze floating through the timbers like she has forgotten I am even there. 'They were good kids,' she says.

'I didn't do it, Lily.' I move in front of her so she has to look at me. 'I didn't kill them.'

'It was an accident, Jenna. Unintentional, however it happened. On that much we all agree.'

I nod. But it was more than just an accident. They would have prosecuted me, except that I was too injured for them to bother. If the police saw me now, what would they do? *But it is still more than that.* It runs through me, trying to connect, bits that are loose. Neuron. Neurochip. *I didn't kill my friends.* Or maybe I just can't accept that I did. Maybe that would mark Jenna's permanent fall from perfection. I gather three scattered books from the floor and stuff them in the box.

Lily stands, holding the flaps shut while I tape it. 'Why are you telling me all this and not your parents?'

I'm surprised she would ask. Is she testing me? We both know the answer.

Because I always have.

I remember the weekends, taking the train to her house. Planning all the things I would share, all the events, worries, and mistakes I kept from Mother and Father. I saved them for Lily, because she would listen. Sometimes a person gets tired of being fixed all the time. Where every little problem becomes a project. Where every shortcoming needs to be addressed. They eventually have to share with someone. My someone was Lily.

'I seem to remember that you had a high tolerance for listening without melting down over the content.' I pull off a last section of tape and stick it to the flap. 'It wears on a person, you know, always having to be perfect. You know that one day something will happen, some problem that won't fit into a neat little project. Something that can't be fixed. Then where does that leave you?'

She doesn't hesitate. 'You become mortal like the rest of us,' she says. She turns away, busying herself with more of the mess I have created. I could almost feel sorry for her. I see the line she is dancing. It is the same one I have danced with ever since I saw blue gel beneath my split flesh.

'You never did tell me,' she says. 'What were you looking for when you turned into a human tornado?'

It is a casual slip, nothing more. I shouldn't attribute much meaning to it, but still, I notice the word *human*. I would gladly be a human tornado.

'Something to wear,' I answer.

'The fedora is something to wear.'

'I was looking for a red skirt I used to have.'

'It must have been some skirt.'

'It was. I bought it when I was shopping with Kara.'

'Oh.' The meaning of the skirt echoes in the single syllable.

'I wanted a change from all the blue shirts and pants I have now. I thought it might be out here, but I guess Claire left all of my stuff in Boston. More appearances, I suppose.'

'Probably something like that.'

I begin sweeping scraps into a dustpan and change the subject. 'And you never did tell me—how did all these boxes end up here?'

'A detour,' she says, frowning. 'Claire called me. The house situation had become a problem. She was frantic. The place they had originally planned on hadn't worked out at the last minute. But then your father had an old childhood friend, Edward, whom he knew he could trust. Edward told him about a place near him that was perfect—the right climate, out of the way, roomy, a little run-down, but otherwise just what your parents needed. Except they didn't want ownership traced to them or your father's business. They were in a hurry, so I was the quickest solution. Claire and I have never had the same last name, and no one keeps tabs on what I do anyway. So I bought it for them.'

'Buying it didn't mean you had to come here.'

'She asked. No, correction. She *begged*. She said she needed me. She was scared. And I figured that no matter what I thought about the whole thing, she is my daughter. My only daughter.'

So Lily is under Claire's spell, too. She's not that different from me.

Lily looks up, squints, then shakes her head. 'Might as well tell you the rest. I was also drafted as part of the escape plan—if it became necessary.'

'*What?*'

'They needed an escape plan in case the authorities caught up with them. So while your parents provide subterfuge, I am to whisk you to Edward, who in turn will help whisk both of us out of the country. The choice was Italy, since they don't have the same restrictive laws as us and the climate would work well for you.'

Whisk me. Like I am a piece of dust deposited in a dustpan. 'Why didn't they just *whisk* me out to begin with?'

'Why do your parents do any of the things they do? They want it all. And if they can get away with it, they will.'

I note her take. Getting away with it. *It* being me, and me being illegal. And now, against her will, she is caught up in something she doesn't believe in and that is against the law. How far will a parent go for a child?

'Well, just where would you be right now if you weren't stuck in this lovely little resort?'

She smiles. 'I was on my way to a friend's villa near Montalcino in Tuscany. A nice enough place to drop out. They offered it to me for as long as I wanted. I was even going to try my hand at winemaking.'

Lily's own little Walden, never realized. For this. 'So you traded an Italian villa and wine for a crumbling Cotswold and an illegal lab pet. You're not very good at trades, are you, Lily?'

She empties a dustpan of broken glass into the trash and looks at me straight on, briefly, then bangs the dustpan against the can to get off all the last particles. 'I do okay,' she says.

The clean-up is done. There is no busyness to keep us here.

We stand there uncomfortably. Our reason for working together has ended, and I still want so much more from Lily. The oafish out-of-step me surfaces, and I cross the thin line we dance.

'Would I have wanted this, Lily? Would the Jenna you knew have wanted what I am now?' In an instant I am desperately afraid because I have crossed a boundary. A black-and-white, yes-and-no one.

'That depends, Jenna,' she says. 'What *are* you now?'

The black-and-white answer I was expecting swirls into murky gray. 'I don't know.'

'Well, until you can answer my question, I can't answer yours.'

Identity

> **Identity** n. *1. The condition of being oneself and not another. 2. The sense of self providing sameness and continuity over time. 3. Exact likeness in nature or qualities. 4. Separate or distinct existence. 5. The qualities of a person that make them different from others.*

I check them off.

Different from others. Is one yes out of five enough?

Lily says percentages and politicians can't define identity, but they've defined mine: illegal lab creation. The hand that I have been dealt. Is this what Allys meant?

Allys is so sure of herself. So confident. She calls Dane a decomposing turd without blinking. Without knowing it, she calls me a lab pet. Why am I so drawn to someone who could destroy me? Why do I need her to be my friend?

The dictionary says my identity should be all about being separate or distinct, and yet it feels like it is so wrapped up in others.

The Unknowable

Are there some things I will never know?

The unanswerable I will have to accept?

Have I changed the way everyone does, time and events
    molding me?

Or am I a new Jenna, the product of technology, changed by
    what was put in or maybe what was left out?

And if my original ten percent really is enough, what if it had
    been nine percent? Or eight?

Is one numeral that different from another?

When is a cell finally too small to hold our essence?

Even five hundred billion neurochips aren't telling me, and I'm
    not sure they ever will.

The question that twists inside me again and again—am I
    enough?—I realize, for the first time, is not just my question,
    but was the old Jenna's question as well.

    And I think about Ethan and Allys and even Dane,
    and I wonder
    has it ever been their own question, too?

Environment

'I'm leaving to pick up your father. I'll be back soon,' Claire calls from the bottom of the stairs.

I hear her leave. The house is empty. Lily has gone to Sunday Mass. I have never been left home alone before. Are they beginning to trust me? I look out the window at the veranda below. The railings have all been replaced and the brick walls repaired. The Cotswold is beginning to look more like a house and less like a ruin. Claire's magic is working. Day by day, it improves. The upstairs rooms remain empty, but they are at least clean now, the spiderwebs all swiped away.

I've been cleaning my own room today. Claire does not employ housekeepers anymore, not like she did in Boston. She does not want prying eyes or ears. When a workman must come inside, she follows him and hovers. Not a minute is given for free wandering.

There is not much to clean. My room is still sparse. *'It is life near the bone where it is sweetest,'* I say to the walls. I amuse myself with my cleverness. I run a cloth over my desk and chair and I am done.

I pick up my copy of *Walden,* now uploaded word for word into my biochips, but there is still something different about opening a real book, the scent that emerges, seeing one word at a time and soaking in its shape and nuance. I wonder about things like the sounds and scents that surrounded Thoreau as he wrote each sentence and paragraph.

Turning pages, feeling the paper, I wonder if any of the trees from Thoreau's forest are still alive and wonder what Thoreau would think today if he could visit my small pond and eucalyptus grove. I wonder if, unlike Thoreau, two hundred years from now I might still be able to visit my pond and forest. When I turn the pages of the book and read the words and the spaces between, I have time to think about these things. Thoughts like these are not written down or uploaded into my Bio Gel. These thoughts are mine alone and no one else's. They exist nowhere else in the universe but within me.

I'm stopped by this new thought. What if I had never had the chance to collect and build new memories? Before I can think what I am saying, I hear myself whispering 'thank you' to the air. I *am* thankful, grateful, in spite of the cost, to be here. Have I forgotten the hell I traveled, or are these new memories a cushion softening its sharpness?

I return *Walden* to the center of my desk and take my dust cloth to my closet to drop it in the laundry bin. Claire will probably be home soon. I glance at the corner of my closet. The key. Almost forgotten. I am chilled again, remembering Father's face when I mentioned it. I bend down and pull back the corner of carpet. It's still there and I snatch it into my fist like it might disappear. I walk to the top of the stairs and lean over the banister.

'Claire? Lily?'

Here! Jenna! I startle, almost dropping the key. I freeze on the landing. Listening. But the house is quiet. Was it only a voice I remember?

I grip the key, stepping on the first stair. I already know what is in Mother's closet. Only computers. But it *was* dark. Maybe there was something else I didn't notice. What would Father be afraid for me to see? Something pounds within me, something at my core, but I know it is not a heart. I take another step, and another, until I am standing at Mother's door.

After the strides we have made, the tender moments we have shared, is this betrayal? I look over my shoulder, back down the long empty hallway. 'Mother?' My voice is strung tight. Hearing it deepens the pounding within. The walls of the hallway pulse with the stillness. I push open her door.

The room is bright, airy, nothing to be afraid of. I walk in, hearing the awkward shuffle of my feet on the floor. *Jenna.* I stop. My breath catches again, and my nails dig into my palm. I step closer to the closet. I remember the worried flash of Father's eyes again, and I thrust the key into the lock, turning the bolt, throwing the door open.

The table is still there.

And the computers.

And the faint green glow.

This time I find the light switch on the outside wall and I push it on. I walk in. The room is ordinary. The walls plain. I look at the floor, the ceiling, under the table. There is nothing else in here but the three computers. Mine is still in the middle, one of the bolts still loose. I step forward and almost touch it but pull back.

I don't remember having my own computer in Boston. But I must have had one because my name is clearly marked on the side panel. The computer is large and oddly shaped, not like any I have ever seen, a six-inch square with two ports, both unused. There is no monitor. This has to be it. This is what they don't want me to see.

I stand there, staring, trying to decide. Trust them. Or trust a whisper inside of me.

If I could get it loose, I could connect it to my Netbook upstairs and see what it contains. I reach down and touch my fingertips to my name. JENNA ANGELINE FOX. My fingers tingle. Why here?

The other two don't have labels. Maybe they are mine, too? I lay my hand on the first one. *Now! Hurry!*

I jerk away. My head pounds. I touch the second computer, wondering at its purpose, and then I squat.

There *are* labels. Faint and hastily scrawled with a pen.

L. JENKINS, and K. MANNING.

What?

My knees buckle and I fall to the floor. What are—How—Why did—My thoughts trip and cut one another off. I stand up and step back, looking at the three oddly shaped boxes. Why would Mother and Father have *their* computers? I run from the closet down the hallway to the kitchen, where Lily keeps a drawer of basic tools. I rummage through for a screwdriver. There is no question now. I know who to trust. I find a large flat screwdriver and run back across the house to Mother's room. Mine first. Then the others. I'll connect them all to my Netbook. I'll upload the contents and see for myself. I'll upload—

I stop midway down the hallway. I see Father's eyes. Mother's desperate glance. A dark locked closet and hidden key. *Upload.*

We cracked the code, Jenna.

The screwdriver slips from my fingers.

Nanobots the size of blood cells are injected, sometimes even without a person's knowledge.

My feet stumble forward.

Think of a glass ball twirling on your fingertip...

The walls sway. Mother's door looms.

The mind is an energy that the brain produces...

I grip the frame of the closet door to steady myself.

You have to keep it spinning or it falls and shatters...

I stare at the three humming boxes.

...we upload those bits of information into an environment that allows that energy to keep spinning...

Correction. Environment. I stare at three humming black environments. Hell.

Hurry, Jenna. Come.

I can't.

I back away.

Backups. Of course.

And I run.

Shared Thoughts

The floor of the forest is damp. The blanket of eucalyptus leaves rustles beneath me. I have been lying here for hours, listening to the sounds. There are few. The leaves swishing beneath me when I turn my head or move a leg. The sighing creak of branches and limbs when the breeze pushes them farther than they want to go. The occasional hollow caw of one raven to another. The faint desperate cry of Claire calling *Jenna*, wondering where I have gone.

I hold my hands above me, my fingers fanning out in a delicate performance, my palms coming together, warm and smooth. It is real skin. Real movement. The structure listens to my neurochips. When I think *clap,* my hands obey, and the frenzied claps echo through the forest. My brain. *I do have ten percent.* The butterfly,

193

Mother called it. My winged bit of humanity. *A few ounces at most.* If I believe in such a thing as a soul, did it take flight with a glistening handful of tissue? Does the soul cling to the last vestige of humanity until there is no more? If a soul can reside in a fistful of embryo, why not in a fistful of white matter?

I cup my palm, imagining a butterfly landing in it, feeling the flutter and life, and I go to a sleeping, remembering dreamworld. I dream of golden-winged butterflies, red skirts, lopsided cakes, and Ethan's mouth on my own.

When I wake, the rickrack of sky visible above the canopy has gone from cerulean to black. The tops of the trees are barely visible, only a sliver of moon to light their edges.

'Jenna!' Mother's distant searching voice is pitiful.

I have to go back. Eventually. But not until I understand one thing. Which is the real me? The one in the closet or the one here on the forest floor?

Backup

They are sitting on the veranda as I emerge from the forest. Leaving the back door open as I ran out must have given them a clue to my direction. In another time, Mother would have called the police by now, but that is not an option anymore. Mother is the first to see me. She begins to stand, but Father reaches out and she sits again. Lily sips a glass of wine.

Walking toward them, I feel like I am interrupting a candlelit dinner party instead of a frightened vigil. Lily passes Mother a platter of stuffed mushrooms. I feel an annoyed ruffle run through me.

'It's a little late, don't you think?' Father says casually. He takes a bite of cheese and then nonchalantly washes it down with a swig of wine. His eyes are angry, glassy, but his movements are practiced restraint.

'Not too late,' I answer.

'We can't keep living this way, Jenna,' Mother blurts out.

Father shoots her a glance. Lily rolls her eyes.

'Welcome home, Father,' I say. I reach out for a mushroom and before anyone can stop me, I pop it in my mouth.

All three stare at me, the impervious Jenna Fox, at the center of attention once again. Where are the cameras? I play the scene with an exaggerated bow.

'Dammit, Jenna!' Father slams his hand down on the glass tabletop, rattling the dishes. 'You're not the first person in the world to have to deal with a disabling accident!'

'I know, Father.' I sit down in the chair opposite him. 'There's those three people in the closet, too. The ones in the black boxes? Now *that's* what I call a disability.'

Lily grunts. 'Touché.' And she downs the rest of her wine.

'Jenna, we have to talk about these things,' Mother says. 'You can't just run off and worry us every time you hit a bump.'

'I didn't hit a bump. You both hid it from me.'

'They aren't people,' Father says.

'Have another,' Lily offers, holding out the platter of mushrooms to me.

'We didn't hide it from you,' Mother says.

'Did you hear me?'

'Behind a locked door *is* hidden.'

'Shall I open another bottle?'

'What do you expect when you're acting like this?'

'Stop!' I yell. I can't keep up with the tangled conversation.

'I'll open another,' Lily says. She shuffles off to the house while we sit at the table, using the silence to regroup. Mother lifts her hair off her shoulders and blows at the wisps on her forehead. The shifting Santa Ana winds have made it unseasonably warm for March. Father turns his glass, suddenly so interested in his wine, his brows creasing, his concentration holding his emotions back. I see his lips pull tight, like a seam within him is splitting.

'Let's start at the beginning,' Mother says softly. 'What were you doing in my closet?'

'Let's start *more* at the beginning,' I say. 'Why is there a computer in your closet with my name on it?'

'It's a backup, Jenna,' Father says, in his usual cut-the-crap voice. 'We had to save the original upload.'

I can hardly see Father as he continues to explain. I can only remember a place with no dimension, no depth, no heat, no cold, but immeasurable amounts of darkness and solitude. Another Jenna is still there.

'We already told you that this is uncharted territory. We don't think anything will go wrong, but if it does, we have a backup just in case. But it can't be a part of any Network. It's too risky. So we keep the bioenvironment completely independent of all Networks and shared power sources.'

I stand, holding my arms, walking in circles, shaking my head.

'Jenna—'

'*What are you doing?* You have another me trapped in that environment! And Kara and Locke!'

Father shifts in his seat. His shoulders hunch awkwardly. 'It's not another you or them, and *trapped* isn't a good word to use. It's only bits of infor—'

'It's a mind. You said so yourself.'

'But it's a mind without any sensory input. It's like limbo or a dreamworld.'

'Trust me, it's not a dreamworld. Not by a long shot. It's more like a nightmare.' I collapse back into my chair and close my eyes.

'Jenna, it's only been a few months,' Claire says. 'Give us some time to work this out. We're still trying to think it through ourselves. That's all we ask. Just give us some time.'

She is not listening. Neither of them are. They don't want to believe that the place I occupied for eighteen months was anything less than a dreamy waiting room. And time is all I've given them. Time. Months. Years. A lifetime of being theirs. Will a time come when I can ever say no? Do I even have time? I need a backup because something could go wrong? I am suddenly aware of my quivering hands and the tremor in my leg.

'What could go wrong?' I ask. It hadn't occurred to me that I could suddenly blink into nothingness like a crashed computer with not even two years used up on my shelf life. That two years seems so precious now—a lifetime. I don't want to be...gone. My insides tighten and I feel breathless. *Breathless* from someone who has no lungs. Should I laugh or cry?

I feel Father grab my hands in his, and I open my eyes. 'We don't think anything will go wrong, Angel. But we don't have any long-term data for a project of this magnitude. The Bio Gel has only been in use for eight years and then it's only been used for isolated organ transplants, not as an entire nervous system.

The problem might be if there are conflicts between your original brain tissue and the Bio Gel, signals that might create almost an antibody effect, with one trying to override the other. We haven't seen it yet and we don't expect to, but scenarios like that are why we have backups. Just in case.'

Blink. Gone.

I don't want to blink out of existence. Images flash through me. Ethan's stormy eyes. Mr Bender's sparrows. Allys smiling. Claire holding her arms out to me. The forest and sky that mesmerized me for hours. New images from my new life. Images that are not in my backup. That's a different Jenna. I want to keep the Jenna I am now.

'Here we go.' Lily plops another bottle of wine down on the table and places an extra glass in front of me.

'Have you lost your mind, Lily?' Father says.

'It's not like she can get drunk.'

'But it still—'

'Leave it, Matt,' Mother says.

'Pour up, Lily,' I say, lifting my glass.

She does, and Father doesn't say another word.

I don't get drunk, but I do feel it warm my insides. However primitive my digestive system may be, it seems to appreciate Lily's effort, even if the wine is tasteless.

'Why are there backups for Kara and Locke?' I ask.

'It was me,' Mother says as she rubs her temple. She takes another sip of her wine and looks out across the pond. 'We had already scanned you. We had hope. But a few days after we moved you, I had to go back to the hospital to retrieve some of your belongings and I saw Kara's and Locke's parents and the agony they were going through. I begged your father to scan them, too, in case they didn't make it.' She sighs and looks back at me. 'So he did.'

I'm ashamed as I look at the pain etched on Mother's face, and yet angry, too, because of a missing scar on my chin and two lost inches and a perspective I will never see from again. The angry me overrides the shamed one. I am entitled, after all, the entitled Jenna. I mix in some sarcasm, too, so I get the full value I have coming to me. 'And where are their new-and-improved bodies?'

'There are none,' Father says. 'Right after I scanned them, the police report on the accident came back and their parents wouldn't even talk to us, much less let us get close to Kara and Locke. Locke died a few days later, and we couldn't even get something as simple as a skin sample. They cremated his body. Same thing with Kara. She was moved to another facility, and we weren't allowed access. We don't even have any original DNA. Nothing to build from. They will never have new bodies.'

I feel sharpness, like a razor is slicing through me, cutting one part away from another, a part that can never be stitched or put back together. Kara and Locke, forever not here or gone. 'How long do you plan on keeping them?'

'We don't know.'

'As long as we can.'

'As long as charges—'

'Indefinitely.'

'At least until—'

'There may come a time when we can use their scans.'

'For the accident. Something they know might help. We have to keep them as long as there is a possibility—'

'Witnesses?' I say. 'You're keeping them as *witnesses?*'

'Not *them*, Jenna. It's only uploaded information.'

Is that all I was? All those months, my thoughts crammed into a formless world? Only bits of information? And if that's all I was then, am I any more than that now? I just have better packaging. Does the ten percent of original brain really matter? My whole brain was scanned and uploaded. The fleshy human handful seems more like a sentimental token. Or does it really communicate my humanity to the neural chips in mysterious ways even Father doesn't understand?

Only uploaded information. Kara and Locke in that dark world forever. Can I live with that?

'Something they know might hurt me, too,' I say. No one comments. We all know that opportunity would never transpire. Anything bad Kara and Locke might have to say about Jenna would never be heard. They are being saved only in case they could help me. I reach out to refill my glass, and Lily stops me.

'You've had enough,' she says.

And I suppose I have.

I look at Mother. Her eyes dart from Father to me and back again, jumping, caught like a hooked fish. Caught between two worlds again. 'It's for you, Jenna.' And now we've come full circle. As we always do.

'Everyone has to die eventually,' I say.

Father lifts the bottle of wine. He holds it in front of the candle to judge its remaining contents. He empties half into Mother's glass and half into his own. He takes a leisurely sip.

'No more,' he says.

Tossing

I don't sleep.

I hold on to my bed.

The backups must go.

My fingers dig into my sheets.

I want sleep. Forget. Melt into night.

But.

What if something goes wrong?

I may need them.

It is only information.

Limbo.

Dreamland.

That's all.

And if I try hard enough

maybe I can forget the dark place where

they

we

are.

Viewpoint

It is a rare day. Rae is teaching a lesson.

In her own way.

I am tired. But fidgety. My lack of sleep did not merit my staying home from school. Mother and Father have a distorted sense of normalcy. 'You wanted to go. You will go. It will be good for you.'

We watch Net News covering a session of Congress. A senator talks. And talks. It is the longest filibuster in history. Senator Harris is breaking the record of Senator Strom Thurmond set back in 1957. No one has been so long-winded—or driven—until now. He has been droning on now for twenty-five hours and thirty-two minutes, one hour and fourteen minutes past Thurmond's record. For this, Rae has commandeered the floor. For this, even Mitch has joined us in the classroom. Mitch mimics Rae's nods, and then sighs so there is no doubt. This *is* historic.

I sit between Ethan and Allys, focused on their presence beside me. I want to lean over and whisper in Ethan's ear in one breath and weave my fingers into Allys's hand in the next, and I don't want to listen to the senator at all. I want to define my place in their worlds and not try to understand the definitions the senator spews forth about his own. Right now I feel the overload—like I could burst in two with needing friendship on one side of me and love on the other. These are the definitions I need to refine.

Dane sits behind me. I feel his tap on my chair. Tap. Tap. I am here. I am here. I am everything. Pay attention. And the senator drones on. And Rae beams. Glows. Historic. Pay attention. Tap.

Tap. Allys. Ethan. I do.

My world is too complicated. People. Politics. Self. The rules of it all. And trying to understand. It feels like a fugue and my drunken fingers are tangled trying to play it. *Play, Jenna. Listen.* The senator glistens. I notice his beads of sweat and handkerchief more than his words. *Now, my fellow citizens. Now. Before it is too late.* I watch Allys more than the senator. She leans forward in her seat. Her head nods. *Yes.* I turn my head to the right. To Ethan. He slinks back. *No. No.*

And Dane taps.

Taps.

Does she like me? Would she if she knew?

The senator swipes his forehead. 'For God's sake,' he cries. 'Do we dare go down that path? My fellow lawmakers. My esteemed senators. Can we take that chance?'

He breathes. A sigh. A period.

There is a roar. An applause. Only a few claps from the senators who are still present and awake. The roar is from Allys. And I am not sure what it is even about because for the last hour I have been consumed with a need that is different from Rae's or Allys's or the senator's, and I am alone in my need, and there is no one who can understand. Being a 'first' doesn't feel so groundbreaking.

'Magnificent!'

'Historic!'

'Boring.' The last, predictably, from Dane.

'Twenty-five hours, forty-six minutes!'

I should have paid attention. When someone speaks for over twenty-five hours, it must be important. It must matter. It matters to Allys.

'Will it make a difference?' Allys asks Rae.

'Of course,' Rae says. 'Maybe not in ways any of us expect. But it will not be forgotten. Every voice leaves an imprint.'

'Especially one that has talked for so long,' Mitch adds.

'But how will they vote?' Allys asks.

'We'll have to wait and see,' Rae answers.

'Vote on what?' I ask.

Allys frowns. I have not paid attention, and she is hurt that something that matters so much to her has slipped past me. I try to make up for it by focusing on Rae's explanation.

'A bill is before Congress,' Rae explains, 'and Senator Harris has been trying to persuade his fellow senators to vote against it. By talking for so long, he has hoped that it will give some chance for the opposition to make a stronger case, sway others to their point of view.'

'What is the bill?' I ask.

Ethan lays his head down on his desk and closes his eyes as Rae explains.

'The bill is the Medical Access Act, which will put all medical decisions and choices back into the hands of physician and patient. It will cut the FSEB entirely out of the process.'

'And he thinks that is bad?'

'Weren't you listening, Jenna? Of course it's bad!' Allys doesn't try to hide her disappointment in me. 'If the FSEB had been in existence fifty years ago, I might not be stuck with all this hardware. My toes might actually feel like toes and not numbed-up sausages! And this isn't just all about me. Look at the Aureus epidemic and the millions who might not have died. And now Congress is trying to limit its power? Next, they'll want them out of all the research labs! God help us if that happens!'

'But,' Mitch says, 'the counterargument is that the FSEB is a bureaucratic financial drain that often impedes lifesaving measures.'

'It's the tech and pharmaceutical companies who are behind it,' Allys says, ignoring Mitch's comment. 'They've been lobbying like crazy. The big ones like Scribtech, MedWay, and especially Fox BioSystems—' *Click*. Allys hesitates for the briefest second, her eyes flickering over me, before she finishes her sentence. Probably a millisecond no one else notices. 'They've poured billions into getting this bill passed.'

And with that last sentence, she sits down. She is suddenly done talking about the bill. Rae continues with the lesson, trying to prod us to share our opinions, but an unexpected blanket has come down on us. Mitch leaves. Rae turns off the Net and says we will talk more after lunch. Maybe food will perk us up.

We walk to the market across the street and sit at our usual corner table. I notice Allys's face is damp, with a dull yellow pallor, while her hands remain a cool, creamy prosthetic peach. When she swallows her pills, they seem to crawl down her throat. She takes another sip of water, trying to coax them down, then another. She stares at me. I stare back. She nibbles at her food, then pushes it away. Ethan looks back and forth between us, his leg jiggling and shaking the table.

'You're Jenna Fox, aren't you?' she finally says.

'Brilliant.' Ethan jumps in much too quickly. 'How'd you figure that out? Maybe from her *telling you* the first day she met you?'

'Don't smooth things over for me, Ethan,' I say. His leg stops jiggling, and he draws in a deep pleading breath.

Allys shakes her head. 'It's all coming together. Most people don't pay attention to that kind of news, but working in the ethics office, I hear it all. I remember something about a daughter,' she says. 'I should have put it together when you told me you were in an accident. You're the daughter of Matthew Fox.'

'Would that make me the enemy?' I ask.

'No...'

'But?'

Ethan shakes his head ever so slightly. 'Jenna,' he whispers.

'They said his daughter was in an accident. One that most professionals believed was not survivable.'

'At least with the FSEB's current point system in place, right?'

'That's right.'

'Well, then maybe I'm not her, after all. Jenna Fox is a common name.'

'Maybe not,' she says. 'Because if you were her, that would mean...' She trails off, deliberately leaving a space for us to fall into. I see it. Ethan doesn't.

'What?' he blurts out. 'You'd have to run to your little squadron of FSEB bureaucrats and report her?'

Allys sits back. Her eyes narrowing on me, then Ethan. She pulls off her prosthetic arm and rubs the stump. It is red and scarred and ugly. 'You give me too much credit, Ethan. I can't run anywhere. I can only hobble. Obvious, isn't it?'

She returns her prosthetic arm to her stump, wincing at the momentary pinch of the magnetic fields that hold it tight. She tests her fingers, one by one. 'I'm beginning to forget, I think. What they ever felt like. It scares me, what science can do.' She pushes away her sandwich. 'I guess, right along with my fingers,

I've lost my appetite.' She stands. Neither Ethan nor I stop her, and she leaves.

I lift my fingers until they are silhouetted against the sunlit window. I test them just as Allys did. One by one. Packaging.

Maybe

'She's going to tell.'

Ethan pulls me close. We are behind the market, knee deep in overgrown grass, sandwiched between forgotten picnic tables and trash bins. He pulled me away when I began to cry, leaving his lunch and curious stares from other customers behind.

I feel his arms stroke my back, his hands tighten around my waist, his breath, and his smell, my tongue warm against his, a stirring inside of me that makes my tongue press farther. Did I ever feel these things before? Do I care? Our kisses are desperate.

My sobs return. Wild. Like an animal. Ethan holds tighter, like he can squeeze away my demons. I push away. 'Why do you care, Ethan? You don't know me.'

His hands drop from my sides. He closes his eyes and shakes his head.

'Ethan,' I whisper.

'I don't know, Jenna.' His eyes are wide again. Glassy. 'I—I feel something. Every time I look at you. Don't ask me to explain it all. Does everything have to have a tidy explanation?'

'I'm not like other girls.'

'I know.'

'Ethan.' I cup his face in my hands. 'You don't know. I'm

beyond different. I'm—'

'Maybe that's what I see when I look at you, Jenna. Someone who will never fit in again in quite the same way. Someone like me. Someone with a past that's changed their future forever.'

'Or maybe it's just that you see me as a second chance. You couldn't save your brother, but maybe you can save Jenna. Justice. Is that what you're looking for?'

He steps away and kicks the loose leg of a picnic table so it tumbles to one side, then he swings around. 'Or maybe I'm a masochist and I like girls who are as annoying as hell! Don't try to analyze me, Jenna. I am what I am.'

And I am what I am. I just need a definition for what that is.

> **Jenna** n. *1. Coward. 2. Possibly human. 3. Maybe not.*
> *4. Definitely illegal.*

'Let's not argue.' Ethan comes up behind me and places his hands on my shoulders. 'Why did you cry back in the market? Are you afraid? We'll talk to Allys. Change her mind.'

'I'm not afraid, Ethan.' At least not of Allys. I'm afraid of my thoughts, my feelings. I'm afraid of my fingers against a sunlit window and the shocking relief that comes with it, when I should feel shame. I'm afraid that I feel wildly alive and grateful and like the Special Entitled Miracle Child Jenna Fox, while boxes sit in a closet trapping minds that will never see fingers or sunlight again, and I am too afraid to let them go because I might need them. I'm afraid of a hundred things, including you, Ethan, because everything in the universe says it's not right, but that doesn't keep me from wanting it.

And I'm afraid I am becoming something that the old Jenna Fox never was and maybe ten percent isn't enough after all. I am afraid of Dane and that the something that everyone says he is missing is the same thing Father may have left out of me, too, and that Senator Harris is perfectly right about it all and Father is perfectly wrong. I'm afraid I will never have friends like Kara and Locke again and it will all be my fault. I'm afraid that for the rest of my two or two hundred years I will still have all these questions and I will never fit in.

And I'm afraid that Claire and Matthew Fox will discover that the new, improved Jenna doesn't add up to three babies at all and never did and everything they risked was for nothing. Because when all is said and done, I am not special at all. Those are the kind of things I am afraid of.

But I am not afraid of Allys.

'She said she liked me,' I say to him. 'She wouldn't tell.'

'I saw her eyes.'

I turn around and lay my head against his chest. I listen to his heartbeat. A real heartbeat.

'We need to talk to her. Soon,' he says.

Sliding

Allys is not at school the next day. Or the next. Should I worry?

I listen for sounds. Knocks on the door. Footsteps.

Sirens tracking me down.

When Mother and Father are gone and Lily is out in the greenhouse, I listen, waiting for the silence of the house to crumble.

I wait for creaks on the stairs, and I wonder what it would be like to be imprisoned again. And then when the silence is long and sustained and I am beginning to believe it will always be there, when a tiny doorway is opened and I am trying to slide through to that place called normal, the silence is broken again.

Not by footsteps. But by a voice.

Hurry, Jenna.

A voice crisp and clear. Not the voice of my past. Not the voice of a dream. The voice of now.

There are no keys flying through the air. No hot glimpses of a night that still escapes me but has changed me forever. No memories of words said in haste. But fresh words that somehow crawl through my scalp until I feel I may be mad.

We need you. Now.

Match

I stomp through our eucalyptus forest, letting my feet come down hard on twisted pieces of bark and twigs, listening to the snap, the crunch, and the sounds I can control. I kick up the woven mat of leaves at my feet and release months and years of decay and send beetles scurrying for cover. The voices are quiet. I slow my pace. Is it guilt speaking to me? Or did Father not understand everything his tampering might lead to? I hear the rush of the creek at the bottom of the incline and the rustle of something else nearby. Birds?

The forest is foreign, an import, Lily tells me. At the turn of the last century, someone thought he could make his fortune raising the timber for railroad ties. As it turned out, the wood was too hard for cutting once it dried, and the groves were abandoned. They spread on their own, sometimes wiping out native species of plants. Lily is not pleased. *Original, native, pure*—these are the words that matter to Lily. And Allys.

I look at the trees that don't belong, brought here through no fault of their own. Their bark is soft velvet, mottled and creamy, and their scent is pungent. The leaves, smooth slices of silvery green, create a thick, lacy carpet on the forest floor. Beautiful but unwanted. What have they crowded out that was more beautiful or more important?

I reach out between two trees, pressing a hand against each, breathing in slowly, closing my eyes, searching for something beyond their bark and branches and second-class status on these hills, searching for something like their souls.

Snap!

Crunch!

My eyes shoot open.

Pain grips my wrist.

'Dane!' I try to pull away, but he holds tight, squeezing harder, watching my face for my response.

'Let go,' I tell him.

His face is no longer empty but instead crackling with something else. It is the only time I have seen his eyes bright and engaged, like he has been plugged in. He doesn't smile.

'Let's go for a walk,' he says.

'I'm not walking anywhere with you, Dane.'

'Why? You prefer boys like Ethan who are dangerous? I could be dangerous.' He pulls me closer, his breathing labored.

I feel his fingers dig into my skin, his blue eyes, pulled to sharp pinpoints, like an animal's, adrenaline-driven, hungry for nothing else but destruction, empty of self and others. Dane, fully flesh and blood, but one hundred percent of nothing.

'Not nearly as dangerous as me. I'm leaving.' I try to pull away.

'*I said* we're going for a walk,' he says, jerking me closer.

'Let's not,' I answer, and my free hand juts forward to his groin. My aim is on the mark, my grip as tight as his. His eyes widen. His fingers tighten on my wrist. My fingers tighten, too. His eyelids flutter, his face reddens.

'I may walk funny, Dane, but Ethan says I have the endurance of a horse. I can stand here all day long. Can you?'

He makes a last effort by twisting my wrist. Pain rips up my arm. In return, my other hand squeezes beyond his limits. He screams out, releasing my wrist. I let go of him, and he falls to his knees, moaning. Besides the revulsion running through me, I feel something unexpected—gratitude. He's shown me how empty a one hundred percent human being can be. Percentages can be deceptive.

His face trembles, and his eyes are sharp and cold looking up at me. He is still trying to catch his breath, and I know I have only a few seconds before he comes at me again.

'Jenna, there you are! Shall we finish our walk?'

Mr Bender comes through the woods, making a show of his golf club, swinging it more than he is using it for balance on the hillside.

'Yes,' I say, leaving Dane to contemplate how much worse a golf club in his skull might feel than my hand in his groin.

Mr Bender and I walk down the incline and cross the creek

where a downed log provides a bridge. 'I was in my yard when I saw you walk into the forest,' he says. 'When I saw Dane follow a short time later, I grabbed my club.'

'Thank you. Between your golf club and my grip, I think he's headed in the other direction by now.' We walk out of the forest and up the path that leads to his house.

'Should we call the police?'

I hesitate. 'No. It wouldn't be a good idea for either of us. I'll be more careful in the future.'

'You shouldn't go into the forest alone. It's not just that criminal. Sometimes there are mountain lions in the area.'

I stop and face him. 'Really, Mr Bender—or should I call you Edward?—we both know I can be replaced as easily as a damaged Netbook. Backups are handy that way.'

He looks almost as stunned as Dane did a few minutes ago. 'How'd you figure it out?'

'The backups or you?'

'Both.'

'I have five hundred billion neurochips, Mr Bender. It wasn't difficult. But Father probably told you about that already.'

Mr Bender nods, looking down. He shouldn't be ashamed. He was Father's friend before he was mine. I resume my pace. 'When you have five times the brain capacity, I guess it's just a matter of time before you start using it.' Details from two-year-old Jenna's brain had surfaced sometime after I saw the old battered aqua car in Mr Bender's garage. 'And I finally remembered an old photo that hung in our brownstone when I was a toddler. It was of Father with his first car. The aqua one he passed on to you.'

Small slips these are, memories they wouldn't expect from a

two-year-old, but my memories don't differentiate—two days, two years, or ten—they are all the same weight and intensity.

'I just found the house for him. I owed him that,' he says. 'I don't know as much as you may think. Your father told me very little.'

'To spare you, probably. The less you know, the less guilty, right?'

He doesn't reply.

'So you kept in touch with him all these years?'

'Not at first, but after a few years I needed that connection. I needed someone who knew me before. So that the rest of my life wasn't invalid. It's more painful to leave your identity behind than most people imagine. Essentially, you've been erased. It doesn't really make sense, I know, but when I finally contacted your dad, he listened and he understood. He was always there for me, from giving me his car when I needed to get away to being there when I needed to talk.'

'You talk often?'

'Maybe once every year or so. Not often. And then we have to be careful. He called me when you were hurt. He was wild with grief. And then he called me again a few days later. He babbled mostly. Thinking out loud. I thought he was drunk at first. Really talking more to himself than me, but I guess he just needed me there to listen. He said he knew he was going to lose you unless he did something...drastic. He didn't tell me what. He just hung up, and I didn't hear from him again until he called about needing a house that was out of the way.'

'So that was your role. Long-distance Realtor.' A slight tilt of his head, and a hesitant nod, makes me remember what Lily said. 'Oh, and you were also the other half of the whisking team,' I add.

'Whisking?'

'Getting me out of Dodge.'

He smiles. 'Right. I'm part of the emergency drill. Your father said he'd rather keep you here since he can easily get medical support if something goes wrong, but if the authorities should find out, your grandmother is to bring you to my house. From there I take both of you to an airstrip not far from here. It's only a short flight over the border into Mexico to another airstrip. And from there you'd fly to Italy. Italy has more liberal laws regarding transplants.'

'And brain uploads? The Italians can't count?'

He is silent.

'Or to make matters simpler, and save you some time, my parents could just pop my backup in the mail instead. Parcel post could take me to Italy, probably for a lot less expense and worry. Or if they really want to splurge, they could overnight me with Air Express. Or they could—'

The rising delirium in my voice makes me stop my rant.

'Come,' Mr Bender says. 'Let's sit and talk for a bit.'

I nod and follow him up the slope to his house and we sit in two chairs on his back porch looking out at the pond and my own house on the other side.

'What's wrong with Dane, Mr Bender?' I ask. 'My friend Allys says he's missing something.'

'I don't know exactly, Jenna, but I think your friend might be right. All I know for sure is that he's trouble.'

'But at least he's legal.'

Mr Bender jogs his chair toward me and leans forward. 'Listen to me, Jenna. There are different kinds of laws. Some are written in books, and some are written in here.' He taps his chest. 'Dane may have the paper kind of legal, but he has none of the kind that's planted inside.'

But how does it get there?

I look at him, his hand still resting against his chest. How does the 'legal' kind get inside? Can it be sewn in by a surgeon with careful stitches?

'What do you see, Mr Bender, when you look at me?'

I watch his eyes, taking in my skin, my face, my eyes. I see him consider every twitch, every blink of my eyes. I can see his every misstep, every considered lie, every return to truth. It's a line he crosses often, and sometimes lies and truth melt into something else. His tongue runs across his lips. He blinks.

Truth. Lie. Truth. The something else. Confusion at what I am?

'Please,' I say.

'I see a lot of complicated things when I look at you, Jenna. A horrible unexpected turn, a second chance, hope—'

I stand. 'Hope for what, Mr Bender? A life where I can never be what I was, and can't even be what I am now without hiding? This is all too hard.'

'Jenna.' He stands and holds my shoulders. 'I'm sorry for what you're going through. I know it's been difficult. Believe me, no one knows as well as I do how hard it is to start over. I think that's why I wanted to help you from the beginning, maybe even when I shouldn't have. I saw the frightened teen I once was when I looked at you.'

He lets go of my shoulders, but I keep looking into his face.

Mr Bender is as old as my father, but I see something in him that is as young as me. Do certain events in our lives leave a permanent mark, freezing a piece of us in time, and that becomes a touchstone that we measure the rest of our lives against?

I feel my fists relax, my joints loosen. 'I think it was good luck that you were my first friend, Mr Bender.'

'First?'

'That's right. Jenna's first friend, AD.'

His eyebrows raise.

'After Disaster.'

He laughs, his curious Mr Bender laugh, and then suggests a walk in his garden.

We reach the circular clearing where he feeds the birds. 'Here,' he says as he removes his jacket. 'I've been borrowing Clayton Bender's identity for thirty years. Let me share it with you for a few minutes.' He places his jacket on my shoulders and then takes my palm and rubs it with his own. 'Turns out that birds have a better sense of smell than most people think.'

We sit on the log bench and he fills my palm with seed, and even though it is only for the briefest moment, a sparrow lands and flies away with a beak full.

'See? They're used to you now. Next time you won't need me.'

I decide that sometimes definitions are wrong. Even if they're written in a dictionary. Identities aren't always separate and distinct. Sometimes they *are* wrapped up with others. Sometimes, for a few minutes, maybe they can even be shared. And if I am ever fortunate enough to return to Mr Bender's garden, I wonder if the birds will see that piece of him that is wrapped up in me.

Listening

The silence
darkness
nothing
please
let us go
Help us
    Jenna.

        We need you.
          Hurry, Jenna.
            We need you.

Screaming. I hear screaming. My own screams. Theirs.

But no one can hear. A place so dark no one can hear. Except me. 'Help! Please! Somebody!'

'Jenna! Wake up!'

Father is holding me. Mother sits at the end of my bed. I am in a place of light and touch again. 'You were dreaming,' Father says, squeezing me.

'No,' I say. 'I was...' *Impossible.* Father's face is lined, tired. Fear. Mother is perched, waiting, her hair a bird's nest.

'You were what, Jenna?'

'I was listening.'

'To what, darling? What?' Mother asks.

'To Kara and Locke. They're calling me. I heard their voices.'

Father brushes my hair from my face and touches my cheek. 'That's impossible, Angel. You were only dreaming. That's all.'

I don't argue. There would be no point. But I didn't dream the voices. I heard them. Fresh and now. Somehow, someway, they found me. They need me.

But I need them, too.

In the flash between darkness and light, between dream-world and reality, I cross a boundary. I remember the accident.

The Accident

Every detail. Sharp, like claws.

It wasn't the Bio Gel, the searching neurochips, or any of the shortcomings of my new self. It was me all along. The grieving me. The shocked me. The in-denial me. But now, Kara and Locke are forcing me to remember.

I sit in the dark, a sliver of light from the hallway slashed across my bed. I listen to the faint wheeze of air entering and leaving my chest. Breathing. A new kind of breathing. Because of that night.

Keys flying in the air.

My fingers outstretched.

My fingers were *throwing* the keys. Not catching them.

'I can't drive, Locke,' I told him.

'You're the only one with a car,' he complained.

'If you don't drive, Jenna, then we don't go,' Kara added. 'We need you!'

'I'm not driving without a license. Besides, my voice commands aren't even programmed into the car yet. I couldn't start it anyway.'

'Kara could drive,' Locke says. 'And starting it's not a problem.

There's an override. You must have a code or keys around here somewhere.'

The kitchen drawer. Where Claire keeps all the extra keys.

I could have pretended I didn't know where they were.

I could have distracted them.

But I didn't.

I opened the drawer and pulled them out.

'Yes!' Locke says and snatches the keys from my hand. He throws them to Kara. They wait for my response. I hesitate. Wondering. Thinking. But not for too long. I nod.

So we went. Kara drove.

I gave her the keys.

I let her drive my car that even I wasn't supposed to drive yet.

Mother and Father were away for the night. Maybe I was eager for a fall, the thing I feared most. I had been easing toward it, testing the water, not sure what I wanted, except not to be everything I knew I wasn't.

It was a party. A stupid one. We were bored. Uninvited. No one knew us. We didn't know any of them. It was crowded. Tight circles of strangers were drinking and smoking, oblivious to us. Crashing the party was a thrill that lasted five minutes. We were about to leave. But then the unexpected happened. A fight broke out. We didn't know what might happen next. We were out of our neighborhood, out of our league. We were scared and we ran. I had the keys in my purse. Locke and I were on one side of the car. Kara on the other. 'Hurry, Jenna! Hurry!' It was dark. I frantically searched the black cavern of my purse for the keys. When I found them, I threw them to Kara, my fingers outstretched, trying to be sure of my aim.

There was yelling. Shouts. We were out of our element.

Panicked. We were only rule-followers pretending to be renegades. Other cars screeched away.

'Go, Kara!' Locke yelled from the back seat.

She did.

When we made it to the highway, the adrenaline that streaked through us subsided and our fear was replaced with laughter. I hadn't noticed that Kara's foot was still firmly on the accelerator. None of us had. The curve came up so fast. She braked, but it was too late. The car spun, hit the graveled shoulder. There were last-minute shouts.

'Turn!'

'Kara!'

'Stop!'

Kara was crying and screaming, desperately turning the steering wheel. We were tossed about, none of us having bothered with seat restraints in our rush to leave the party. The car skidded, then rolled when the shoulder turned to cliff, a blurred, chopped nightmare where sound and light cut through us. I was screaming, flying. Tumbling. Glass sprayed like a thousand knives, and the world had no up or down. The fear was so complete it webbed together our screams and motion. Blinding white heat and light. Flying free and the sickening thud of my skull on soil. Or was it Kara I heard, landing next to me? And then the sudden sharp contrast of quiet sounds, like tinkling crystal. Dripping. Hissing. A drawn-out crackle. And soft moans that seemed to hover in the air above me. And finally just blackness.

I never saw Kara and Locke again.

I heard them. For a few seconds I heard their breaths, their sighs, their screams. I heard them. Like I do now.

And for all those months, in the dark place where I waited to be reborn, not knowing if I would ever see light again, between my own voiceless cries and pleading, those were the sounds I heard over and over again, the hellish sounds of Kara and Locke dying.

Self-preservation

They are my witnesses. They alone know that I didn't drive.

Someday, sometime, someone will come for me. And I will have Kara and Locke to help me. Save me.

I can keep them.

The entitled Jenna.

How bad could it be to exist in a box forever?

The Last Disc

The cut-glass panes of the living room cabinet prism my reflection into a dozen distorted pieces. I search those pieces, the borrowed blues, reds, and violets, blended with glimmering flesh. I look for a shine, a difference. But I see nothing that says I am different from Dane.

Versions of me and my friends are trapped where I never want to go again. And I won't help them. Blues. Reds. Violets. Flesh. Fragments. Almost human. The same reflection Dane might have.

I turn from the cabinet and go to the credenza that takes up a large portion of the living room wall. I rummage through the drawer, looking for Year Seven / Jenna Fox, the year where I can watch a girl who was still a child and didn't know about expectations. A year when blue birthday cakes and surprises were all that mattered. Year Seven, probably the last year before I knew I was special.

Mother has straightened the drawer and the disc is not where I left it. I run fingers along the file of discs, searching for it, when I notice something else. The camera. It is at the back of the drawer in a space that has been saved for it, but it has been jarred. A disc has partially popped out. I reach in and pull it loose and look at the label.

JENNA FOX / YEAR SIXTEEN—DISC TWO

It shakes between my fingers. This is the last disc. The real last disc.

This is the one Lily wanted me to watch.

A Recital

Jenna floats across the stage. Her movements are precise. Her arms are curved in a graceful arch. Her feet pointing, her legs extending, *arabesque, Jenna*...

...*chassé, jeté entrelacé*...

...*plié*...*pas de bourrée, pirouette, Jenna.*

All at perfect angles, perfect timing. She raises *en pointe*, her balance pure elegance.

But her face is dead. The performance is all in her arms and legs and muscles, and none of it is in her heart.

I remember that night, the feel of the slipper, the ribbon snug at my ankles, the tight bodice of my costume that showed off my perfect tiny waist, the moisture forming at the nape of my neck. I remember before I even see it repeated on the disc. I remember looking out into the audience that night, my performance almost complete, and seeing Lily in the second row and the disappointment in her eyes and how that shook me and gave me permission all at the same time for what came next. *Relevé, relevé.* My well-trained muscles and bones were speaking to me, ordering me to perform. *Relevé, Jenna.* But I was frozen. The music passed me by. *Relevé, Jenna!* The audience is fidgeting. Uncomfortable. Hoping that the moment can be salvaged. I'm not sure it can. I am looking at Lily's eyes on me, but I am seeing us at her kitchen counter just a few days before. I was complaining about my upcoming recital.

'Who are you, Jenna? How can anyone know if you don't show them?'

'I'm tempted. Just once I'd like to let it out.'

'And what would you do?'

'While I was there onstage, I'd move in all the ways I've dreamed of. I'd stomp and grind and swing my hips and show them all.'

'So what's stopping you?'

I remember she was serious, and I remember looking at her like she was crazy. *'It wouldn't be appropriate. I'd let too many people down.'*

'You mean your parents. I think they'd live.'

The audience is holding its breath. The music has stopped.

Relevé, Jenna! My muscles are demanding action.

Stomp! Grind, Jenna. Swing your hips!

And then I feel it. My calves stiffen. My heels lift. *Relevé.* And then a quick hop to *en pointe.* Hold. Hold. Down to fourth position, *plié*, and bow. The audience heaves a single sigh of relief, even though I am completing my dance long after the music has stopped. Their zealous applause erases the gap.

I have delivered. That is all that matters.

Pieces

A bit for someone here.

A bit there.

And sometimes they don't add up to anything whole.

But you are so busy dancing.

Delivering.

You don't have time to notice.

Or are afraid to notice.

And then one day you have to look.

And it's true.

All of your pieces fill up other people's holes.

But they don't fill

your own.

The Beach

'Over here!' Claire calls, waving her arm.

Lily waves back. Neither of us move, and Mother resumes her walk through the tide pools. The ride to the beach was tense. We hardly talked in the car. Mother insisted we go, saying the unseasonably warm March day was perfect for a walk at the beach.

'She needed this,' Lily says.

'I didn't.'

Lily pulls her sweatshirt over her head and ties it around her waist. 'Then what *do* you need, Jenna?' Her voice is sharp.

I look at her and knot inside. I can't answer. I shake my head and walk away. She grabs my arm and spins me around. 'I asked you something. What do you need?'

I pull away. How dare she treat me like a—

'I need—I need—' I want to spit my words into her stupid face is what I need to do, but they just keep catching, like they are snared on something inside. I stand there, my lips still searching for words.

'Tell me!' she says.

I can't.

She lets go of my arm and sighs. 'And that has always been your problem, Jenna,' she says softly. 'You've always been two people. The Jenna who wants to please and the Jenna who secretly resents it. They won't break, you know. Your parents never thought you were perfect. You did.'

What is she talking about? I never thought—'They placed me on a pedestal from the day I was born! What choice did I have but to be perfect! And if I lagged in math or soccer or navel gazing, they got me a personal tutor! And then I was tutored and coached until I *was* perfect! I've been under a microscope my entire life! From the moment I was conceived, I had to be everything because I was their miracle! That's what I had to live up to every day of my life! How dare you say that it was me when it was them! I was conceived to please!'

'What's going on?' Claire asks, running over to see why our voices are raised.

Lily's eyes hold on to me, like she is talking me down from a ledge. Her voice is low. 'Start small,' she says. 'I'll ask again, what do you need?'

'I need...' The words are dammed up. *Start small.* 'A skirt. A red skirt!'

'What?' Claire's confusion is obvious, but her eyes are intense and clear, focusing on me like I am the whole Pacific Ocean.

'And room. I need room.'

Claire looks at Lily. 'What is going on?'

'Listen,' Lily says. She grabs Claire by the shoulders and turns her to face me. 'Just listen.'

'I don't want to be your miracle anymore. I *can't* be your miracle anymore. I need to be here on this planet with the same odds as everyone else. I need to be like everyone else.'

I slow. I take a breath. 'I can't ever be really alive if I can't die, too. I need the backups. Kara's, Locke's... and *mine.*' Mother's face is frozen like I am speaking babble. 'I want to let them go,' I whisper. She doesn't move. 'Destroyed,' I clarify, raising my voice, so that for once my intentions can't be twisted.

Her face loosens, goes blank. She says nothing for much too long.

Now it is me, frozen, and Lily, waiting, wondering if anything I said made it through to her. And then the part in her lips closes and her shoulders pull back. 'We'll stop on the way home and get you a red skirt,' she finally says. She turns and walks away, only pausing for a moment to shoot Lily a stiff, cold stare.

Calculations

The ride home is quiet. I watch Lily. Mother. I see their eyes, unfocused, staring at the road ahead but not seeing it. Each of us are bound by our own thoughts, seeing the edges of our limits, maybe seeing the edges of others'. How far can we push? How far can we bend? How much can we preserve? How can we get what we want? The calculations are endless, not knowing the future, not knowing how far is too far for any of us. My thoughts drift, search, calculate, remembering, jumping to the past and back again.

My baby, my precious baby, I'm so sorry.

The hospital room is dim. Her chair is pulled close. She rocks, hums, whispers, and she smiles. The smiles are the hardest to watch. They are beyond her strength, but somehow she makes them come forth.

Let me die.

Please.

I screamed the words. Over and over. But only in my head. The words couldn't get past my lips. But even as I pleaded within, hoping some message would get across, I knew. As I lay there in the hospital bed, unable to move or speak, as soon as I looked into Claire's eyes, I knew.

She would never let me go.

So much strength within her, but not the strength to let go.

I was forever her baby. Forever her miracle.

How long is forever?

Grasping

Forever adv. *1. Without ever ending, eternally: to last forever. 2. Continually, incessantly, always.*

There are many words and definitions I have never lost.

But some I am only just now beginning to truly understand.

Moving

Lily swings her door shut and heads off to her greenhouse, to simmer, I presume. Father is standing on the walkway talking to someone. He lifts his hand and waves but returns to his conversation. I am startled to see a visitor, since we have never before had one. The visitor's back is to me, but his girth is oddly familiar. Mother gathers two bags of groceries we stopped for on the way home. We didn't get a red skirt. It's not important. It never really was.

'Come in the back way with me, Jenna,' Mother says. Her voice is near an edge I have already calculated. How far can I push? I turn, leaving her at the garage entrance, and walk around to the front where Father talks to the visitor. They are close, keeping their words tight, like the air itself might snatch them up. Father glances at me, willing me to hurry in the door. But I linger, of course.

Tomorrow . . .

Not safe . . .

I concentrate, trying to decipher the whispered words. I detect a rush within me, an ache, and then a stillness, like the words are being whispered right into my ear. Like every available neurochip has been called to task. And they have. I have billions of available neurochips.

They're too vulnerable where they are.

I have several possibilities. By tomorrow I'll move them.

It can't be—

Traced. I know. I have it covered.

And secure.

Have I let you down yet?

She's my life, Ted.

The visitor shakes Father's hand, then turns, knowing all along that I have been watching them both. He nods in my direction, and I feel everything drop within me. He is the tourist from the mission. The one who took Ethan's and my picture.

He leaves, shuffling down the walk and sliding his wide girth into a small car that wheezes under his weight.

'Who is he?' I ask Father as he approaches me.

'It's not important,' Father answers. 'Let's go inside.'

'I've seen him before.'

Father frowns, knowing I won't let it go. 'My security specialist. He takes care of . . . things.'

'Like me?'

'Sometimes.'

'He took my picture at the lavanderia.'

'Not you. He was investigating Ethan and the community project at the mission. Making sure the risk factor was minimal.'

'Is that what my life is now?'

'What?'

'A controlled risk-free cocoon for your lab pet?'

Father sighs and runs his fingers through his hair, the only nervous habit I have observed in him. 'Let's not dig that up again, Jenna.'

'What's he moving?'

Father looks at me, making his own calculations, studying my face and especially my eyes. Does he know I can see lies as plainly as a deep breath or shrug? He doesn't answer. He's catching on. He knows I am becoming more than he planned. More than the endlessly compliant fourteen-year-old he loved. But all children grow up.

'I'll figure it out,' I say.

He concedes. 'The backups. A closet in a house is no place for them. We didn't have time for better choices before, but now we do. He is going to move them to a safer location.'

He stares at me, too close, too carefully, like he is reading every breath and shrug from me as well. I carefully look up to my left, like I am weighing what he has told me, and slowly I look back at him. 'Oh,' I say. 'That's probably a good idea.' He watches, and gradually I see his muscles loosen and relax. He believes me. But that is nothing new. He always did because I was a rule-follower. I played by the rules he understood. But there are new rules now, ones he doesn't know yet. He'll learn. Just as I am learning.

He opens the front door. 'You coming in?'

'No,' I tell him. 'We were late getting back. Ethan is picking me up soon.'

'It's not a school day.' He implies a question. He's become more like Claire than I remember. When did he start clinging to me so? But I sense the answer lies somewhere between the darkness and the fear, sometime when it looked like I would be gone forever, the accident that didn't just change me, but made them both different, too; that was when he changed. Calculations and maneuvers drain from me. I am seven years old and leading him to a cake that is filled with my love for him. I lean forward and kiss his cheek. 'Our friend Allys is sick. She hasn't been to school in days. We're going to see her.'

A simple kiss on the cheek and his eyes are glassy. 'Be home before dark,' he says. I don't answer because lying is not in me right now. But I will try. Because of his eyes. Because I am his life. Because some things don't change.

I stand at the curb, waiting for Ethan, skimming back through the whispered conversation between Father and the stranger. *By tomorrow.* That's what he said. By then the backups will be whisked away. But will their voices? Will I still hear them calling to me, pleading for release? If they only had a second chance, but they'll never have a rebirth, not like me. Their purgatory will go on and on, and somehow they'll always know that I could have saved them. Should have saved them.

When tomorrow? Did he say?

Sometime tomorrow Kara's and Locke's futures will be cemented, and I will become something less than genuine, like the first in a numbered series of art prints. Kara, Locke, and me, forgotten in a storage facility.

Mother and Father won't be going anywhere between now and tomorrow. There's no chance I could sneak into their closet.

Witnesses. They are witnesses.

I don't have the key to the closet anymore anyway. I was stupid to leave it in the lock when I ran out. I can't do anything for them now. *Relevé, Jenna. Relevé.*

I look at my hands. Trembling. A battle between neurochip and neuron, survival and sacrifice.

Where's Ethan? He's late!

I stand on tiptoe, like that will help me see farther down our street. My breaths come in rapid shallow pants, and I feel betrayed by this body that remembers panic with ease but needs coaxing to remember friends. *I can't let them go.*

I spot Ethan's car, finally, turning the corner at the end of our street.

'I can help you.' I jump and turn around. It is Lily.

I don't need to ask. I know what *help* means.

'You have a right,' she says, 'at least to your own backup. And maybe more. Only you know what it's like. If you really want this, we can figure something out—'

Ethan stops his car at the curb. I open the door but look back at Lily. 'They're taking them away tomorrow.'

'Then maybe we'll talk tonight?'

I nod, wondering at her unexpected proposal. 'Maybe we will,' I answer, and I get into Ethan's car.

They Know

'You're shaking.'

'Just my hands.'

'No, all over.' He pulls me close with one arm while he drives with the other. I notice my shoulders trembling for the first time. I try to make it stop, but I can't control them. Is this what

Father talked about? *If there are conflicts with your original brain tissue...signals that might create almost an antibody effect...one trying to override the other...that's why we have backups. Just in case.*

Ethan leans over, one eye on the road, and rubs his lips against my temple. It sends a current through me and, for at least a moment, disconnects me from my thoughts. 'It's okay,' he says. He straightens, returning his full attention to the road, but continues to rub my shoulder. I look at him, wondering how someone so gentle could ever swing a bat into someone else's skull. Do we all have surprising capacities hidden within us? 'Don't worry about Allys telling. She's been out for four days. If she had told someone, we'd know it by now.'

'Maybe,' I answer. 'Or maybe not. You said the FSEB is a bureaucratic machine. My guillotine order may just be delayed in paperwork.'

He's silent, but his eyes dart back and forth across the passing landscape, like he is reading words that are hidden from my view. He rubs my shoulder more vigorously. Finally he blurts out, startling me, *'The greater part of what my neighbors call good I believe in my soul to be bad, and if I repent of anything...'* He pauses, waiting.

I smile and concede. '*...it is very likely to be my good behavior.*'

'*No way of thinking or doing, however ancient, can be trusted without proof. What everybody echoes...*'

'*...or in silence passes by as true today may turn out to be falsehood tomorrow.*' I put my hand up to stop another quote from leaving his lips. 'Ethan, I truly appreciate the effort, but I can recite Thoreau all day long and still be afraid.'

'But maybe I can't,' he says. He squeezes me. 'And feel. Your

235

shoulders have stopped shaking. Guess you don't know as much as you think.'

I notice. The trembling is gone. Afraid but calm. It's a slightly better place to be. I think of the wild energy of cyclones, but at their center is a tiny circle of calm. That is what Ethan has given me. I lean in closer to his shoulder. 'Maybe she's not sick. Maybe she just doesn't want to see me.'

'She didn't look good the last time we saw her. Her color. Something about her was off.'

It's true. I remember noticing her yellow pallor and the way her pills stuck in her throat. Another virus? It couldn't be, not again, but of course, deep down, I know it's possible. Deadly viruses are the plague of our age.

The road to Allys's house dips and weaves. It's a road I have not yet traveled on. It winds deeper and deeper inland, getting narrower, the trees choking the road. Is this really a place I want to go? Does Ethan really know the way?

'She lives this far?'

'Not so far. It only seems that way when you haven't been somewhere before.'

He turns down an impossibly narrower lane. The road is uneven, not quite paved, a mixture of heavy gravel pressed into dirt. It is not a road on which I can picture Allys walking. No homes can be seen from the road; tall scrubby bushes obscure the view. We arrive at a driveway, marked by a simple white post with an address. Ethan maneuvers his truck down the narrow path and we are swallowed up by overgrown oleander, pink and white blooms brushing our windows. It is a cheery contrast to our reality and the reason we are traveling such a long and unknown road. The flashing of white, pink, and green briefly transfixes me.

Our tunnel finally opens up to a large expanse, an emerald lawn skirting a small gray house with a deep shady porch. It is a silent house, still, like it is waiting to breathe, and I brace myself against the seat.

'Maybe no one's home.'

'They're home,' I say. Which neurochips are already reaching beyond what my neurons know? How are they telling me? Or is it simply what they call intuition? But I know with precise certainty. We are being watched. Eyes size up our car.

We park on the circular drive and walk up the porch steps. Ethan's heavy boots boom against the silence. Even birds are afraid to chirp.

I hesitate on the last step. 'I'm not sure—'

'I don't feel good about this either.'

My imagined stomach catches. 'She's our friend.' It's a question as much as a statement.

'I'm not reassured,' Ethan answers.

The door opens before we can knock.

'Is Allys home?' Ethan blurts out.

A woman stares at us, her face blank and her eyes dark and circled. 'I remember you,' she says. The hollowness of her eyes reminds me of Mother when I looked up from my bed in the hospital in those days that I traveled a thin line back and forth between life and death, days where she never left my side. 'Ethan,' the woman finally adds.

'Yes, I picked Allys up once for school.'

'That was kind of you.' Her gaze drifts away like she is recalling an important moment.

'And I'm Jenna,' I say, holding my hand out.

Her focus jerks back, her pupils small, hard beads. 'Jenna,' she says, like she knows who I am. She looks at my outstretched hand and slowly reaches out and holds it. She runs her thumb along my knuckles like she is counting each one, and then she doesn't let go. I look at Ethan, afraid to pull away. She sees us exchanging glances and drops my hand. Her back stiffens. 'Allys isn't well,' she says.

'May we see her?'

A hand reaches around the door and pulls it open wide. 'Why not?' a man says. He is clearly as spent as the woman, the circles under his eyes and the lines of his forehead speaking of days of no sleep.

'She might not be up to it,' the woman protests, blocking the way.

The man's voice is tender, barely a whisper, a short knife in the tension that grips the house. 'They're her friends, Victoria. If not now, when?'

She steps aside. 'This way,' he says. My feet don't move, but Ethan's nudge at my elbow overrides a flurry of thoughts to flee. We follow him through the entryway and down a long hall. I sense the woman's presence close behind, watching our moves. *My* moves. Before we reach the last room on the left, I stop.

I can already smell death. Memories shake me. *Smell.* It was my last connection with this world before I was swept into a dark empty one. It is distinct, sweet and yeasty, the smell of death, like spoiled bread, damp and swollen, coating walls, nostrils, skin, anything within reach, trying to tag it all. Even when I could no longer see, I could still smell death crawling over my skin.

'She's in there?' I ask.

'Yes,' her father whispers. 'It's okay. She'll want to see you.'

238

We take two more steps. Before we can even see her, we can see medical equipment jamming the room. Suction pumps. Trays of gauze, minty mouth swabs, cups of crushed ice, and stacks of white towels.

Ethan steps back and steadies himself against the wall. 'She's too sick to be here. Why isn't she at a hospital?'

Her mother answers from behind us. 'Allys is assigned to Comfort Care only. Her liver is shutting down. And her lungs. Heart. Kidneys. Shall I go on? Pretty much all of her organs are in some stage of failure. And on top of that, her condition has triggered systemic lupus. Her body is basically attacking itself.'

'What about a transplant?' Ethan asks.

'Which organ? She has too many involved. The numbers add up fast. They said she is beyond saving.'

'There was damage when she had her last illness,' her father adds. 'We knew that. But they thought medications would control the damage. She was doing so well. We thought . . .'

He breaks. I watch him sob, hang on to the wall, wiping his eyes, embarrassed, and then looking down, pinching at the bridge of his nose. His shoulders quake and soft moaning breaths escape as he tries to suppress his grief. I have never seen my own father sob. But now the soft breaths of this man cut through me, weaken me, and I fear I may fall to my knees. These are sounds I have heard before. The sounds of a grown man crying when there is nothing left to do. The sounds of my father.

I grab Ethan's arm and pull him into the room. Allys turns her head as we enter. Ethan can't suppress his reaction. 'Oh, God.'

'You're no prize either, Ethan.' Her voice is raspy and weak.

'Allys,' I say. She is small, sunken into sheets and pillows, like she is already half swallowed up by another world. Except for her right arm, her prosthetics are gone, stored away. Her stumps barely peek from her gown. An oxygen tube lies across her upper lip, and a large patch is pressed against her chest.

'Come closer,' she says. 'It's hard to talk.'

Ethan goes to one side of her bed, and I, to the other. 'We didn't know you were so sick,' he says.

She smiles, her lips a weak yellow smear across her face. 'That's an understatement. I'm dying. When organs start shutting down, it doesn't take long. I always knew it was a possibility. My parents were in denial.' She makes an effort at a chuckle. 'Maybe I was, too.' She coughs, her face wincing in pain from the effort. She presses a button on a pad near her fingertips. The patch on her chest clicks. 'Sweet elixir,' she says and smiles.

'Allys, is there anything we can do?' I ask.

'No, Jenna. It's all been done. This little train was set in motion decades ago by people who thought they were above the system. It will probably take decades more to stop it. Only the FSEB can fix this mess we've made. But it's too late for me. With everything I would need, my numbers would be way over the top. It's the law, remember?'

I am silent. For someone so sick, her voice is amazingly harsh.

'Hold my hand,' she says.

Ethan reaches out.

'No. Jenna. I want Jenna to hold my hand.'

Ethan and I look at each other. How can you deny a dying person a simple wish? I reach across her bed and take her prosthetic hand. 'Your hand is so soft. Much softer than mine.' She touches gently at first, then squeezes hard. She pulls at me.

'Closer,' she says. I lean down until my face is close to hers, her sweet, sickly breaths hot against my cheek. She pushes up as far as her left stump will allow, and she whispers into my ear.

She lets go and falls back into her pillow, and I step back.

'What's the secret?' Ethan asks.

'It's not a secret,' she answers and then closes her eyes, her sweet elixir doing its job for another fifteen minutes.

Ethan swipes at one eye with the heel of his hand and clears his throat. 'We should go,' he says.

We say good-bye, but Allys has already fallen asleep.

Her father walks us to the door. His composure is regained. He has returned to the tired man who greeted us, a circle of calm of his own making. 'Thank you for coming,' he says. 'I know it meant a lot to her.'

Her mother hurries out to the porch before we leave. 'You. Jenna. You live on Lone Ranch Road, don't you?'

'Yes.'

'I thought so,' she says. She turns without saying anything else and goes back into the house.

Ethan and I leave, retracing the steps that brought us here. We don't speak until we get out to the main highway.

'I guess it's moot at this point,' Ethan sighs.

'What's that?'

'Allys won't be telling anyone about you now.'

I stare out the window. The landscape sweeps past as a gray blur because I am focused on a distance somewhere between the window and the world around me. An inexact distance that holds nothing but Ally's words. Ethan underestimates her. 'She already did,' I tell him. 'That's what she whispered to me. That's what she meant. It's not a secret. She told her parents. She told them to report me.'

A swath of red flushes Ethan's face beneath his eyes and his hands tighten on the steering wheel. 'I won't take you home,' he says. 'You can come to my house. Anywhere. I'll take you somewhere where no one will find you...'

Ethan continues his desperate plans for my escape, but I find myself drifting, wondering where Ethan's *anywhere* might be, caught up in a world of maybes and what-ifs and wanting to stay there because it is a much safer world for me than the one I am in.

Leaving and Staying

I almost could.

I could almost leave and never look back.

Like Mr Bender, I could leave everything I was behind,
including my name.

Leave because of Allys

and all the things she says I am.

Leave because of all the things I am afraid that I will never be
again.

Leave, because maybe I'm not enough.

Leave because Allys, Senator Harris, and half the world knows

better than Father and Mother and maybe Ethan, too.

Leave.

Because the old Jenna was so absorbed in her own needs

that she said yes when she knows she should have said no,

and the shame of that night

could be hidden in a new place behind a new name.

But friends are complicated.

There is the *staying.*

Staying because of Kara and Locke and all that they will never be
except trapped.

Staying because for them, time is running out and I am their last
chance.

Staying for the old Jenna and all she owes Kara and Locke
and maybe all the new Jenna owes them, too.
Staying because of ten percent and all I hope it might be.
Staying because of Mr Bender's erased life and regrets.
Staying for connection.
Staying because two of me
is enough to make one of me
worth nothing at all.
And staying because maybe Lily *does* love the new Jenna
as much as the old one, after all.
Because maybe, given time, people do change,
maybe laws change.
Maybe we all change.

A Plan

I have an advantage.

At four A.M. in the blackness of my room, I can still see. The hall light has been strategically disabled. I stand behind my door, two hours before the appointed time, because I am a horse and do not tire.

And because I can't sleep.

Fear is caffeine running through my veinless body, jumping from biochip to biochip, circling around my preserved ten percent, my brain, only a butterfly no larger than the real thing, but the most important piece of acreage in my universe. The difference between staying and leaving. I do not tire, but I catch my breath again and again. *Betrayal. Loyalty. Survival. Sacrifice.* They battle within me.

Five A.M.

Fifty minutes to go. Is it too late to change my mind? Would the old Jenna have jeopardized her future for the sake of someone else? I lean close to the wall, the open door sandwiching me, touching my toes. In the dark, they will never see me. I play out the plan for the hundredth time and then I hear a creak on the loose floorboard outside my door and my remembered heart flies to my throat. Footsteps moving into place.

I don't need to look at my clock. My neurochips know to the second how much time has passed. It is time. My breaths come in gulps, and in an instant I curse and cherish neurochips that remember and mimic too much.

Twenty minutes until dawn. Now. It's time. I shake my fingers.

Betrayal. Loyalty.

Survival. Sacrifice.

Choose, Jenna.

I scream. Loud and long. I cry out.

I listen.

I hear doors bang. Swearing. A yell. Footsteps.

I scream again. *'No ... stop ... help!'* Loud so it vibrates from the walls.

Two pairs of footsteps pound up the stairs calling, 'Jenna!'

Two pairs of footsteps running down the hall. Seconds from my door and an empty bed.

Father curses the light that is out.

Seconds.

Through the door. To the bed. An empty bed.

And I slip out.

The door slams behind me. Lily jumps from the darkness and, in a swift, practiced movement, inserts and turns the key.

The locked door that was supposed to shut me in *just in case* now holds them, just in case.

'Hurry,' Lily says, handing me another key. 'You may not have much time. I'll try to explain, calm them down. But you know how they are. Your father may rip this door from its hinges.'

The banging and yelling have already started. I touch the door. 'Try to understand,' I say.

'Jenna! What are you doing? Let us out!'

'Are you okay? What's wrong? Jenna!'

The door quivers with my father's shoulder.

'Go,' Lily says. 'Hurry.'

I take the stairs two at a time, my clumsy feet stumbling twice, my hand gripping the railing to keep me from a free fall. I tumble to the floor at the last stair, scrambling on all fours as I right myself. I run down the hall and grab the crowbar just inside Lily's door that she left as promised, and then I burst into Mother and Father's room, letting the door bang into the wall. My fingers shake as I try to maneuver the key into the closet lock. *It won't go in! Is it the wrong one?* Mother's and Father's pounding rattle the house. I can hear Mother as clearly as if I were standing next to her. Her orders, her pleading, and finally her frantic realization, stab at me. My legs weaken. *Hurry, Jenna!*

'God, let it fit!' I cry, shaking and twisting the key. It slides in. I sob and turn the lock, and the door swings open.

'I'm here, I'm here,' I say, feeling perilously out of control. *Think. Slow down.*

I lift the crowbar like a club. Which one first?

I lower the bar and slide it beneath the bracket on the first backup. Kara. It doesn't budge. *Please.* I heave my full weight on it, and the rivets pop loose. The bracket flies into the wall and down to the floor.

The second one. Locke. Three tries, and the rivets break loose.

And finally the third one. Jenna. I touch the top of the backup, and a dizzy wave overwhelms me. *Hurry, Jenna! Now!* I slide the bar beneath the bracket, and with all my strength, I bear down with a single swift push. The bracket flies loose on the first try.

I remember every detail Father told me about the backups. Once I remove them from their power docks, they will only stay viable for thirty minutes. The special environment that holds them will stop spinning and will let them go.

Let them go.

Where?

Can I do this? What if...

My hands shake as I force them down to lie on Kara's backup.

Please, Jenna.

My fingers surround the six-inch-square box. Small, finite, and yet as infinite as a black hole in a galaxy. The terror and solitude of that empty world flood back to me and I pull away.

Never, Father said. *Nothing of their humanity was left. They will never exist beyond the six-inch cube.*

I hear the moans of an animal. Grieving.

My own cries.

I lay my hands on Kara's and Locke's backups. 'I'm sorry,' I sob. 'I am so sorry.' I pull them from their power docks. 'It won't be long.'

I look at the third backup. Mine. *What do you need, Jenna? What? What?*

I need to own my life.

I pull it loose and cross an invisible boundary from immortal to mortal.

'This is the beginning,' I whisper. *The real beginning.*

I gather the backups in my arms. Waiting here for thirty minutes is too risky. I understand about risk management, too. Mother and Father are resourceful when it comes to me. One thin door won't hold them for long. It's time to complete the plan. The backups need to be somewhere safe where they can't be reached for at least thirty minutes.

I hear a loud crack. Lily yells from above. 'Jenna!' She doesn't have to tell me. Father is determined.

I run down the hallway and yell as I pass the staircase, 'Tell them to look out my window!'

I hurry through the kitchen out to the veranda and down the slope to the pond. Dawn is fingering through the trees and rooftops. I climb onto the granite rock at the edge of the pond and look back at my house. Mother and Father are at my window, throwing up the sash.

'Jenna, no!'

'For God's sake, no!'

I take Kara's backup in my right hand. 'You're free,' I say, and I throw it in the air, a soaring bird in a violet sky. It descends and splashes into the middle of the pond, ripples and spray exploding the quiet glass. Locke's backup follows, falling not too far from Kara's, the low ripples of the two meeting, intertwining, and gently fanning out to become nothing at all. Gone.

I take the third backup into my hand. There are no screams from the window behind me. Acceptance? The final stage of grief? It's over. They know it. And I know it. The final fall of Jenna Fox. A mere girl, like any other.

The cube flies from my hand, high into the sky, and it seems to hang there for a moment, almost suspended, free, and then it falls, disappearing from this world and joining another.

I hold my breath, waiting.

There is no fanfare. The sun doesn't stop its ascent. The coot hens are only mildly disturbed at the brief intrusion and circle back to the cattails to resume their breakfast. One small changed family doesn't calculate into a world that has been spinning for a billion years. But one small change makes the world spin differently in a billion ways for one family.

And for me. The *only* Jenna Angeline Fox.

I sit on the rock's edge watching the ripples lose their bulk and energy. But gone? Who can explain where energy goes? The pond returns to glass. On the surface it may look the same again, but it is forever changed by what lies within.

I hear footsteps. Soft. Slow. They stop behind me. Lily's footsteps.

'I let them out,' she says.

'I should go in.'

'They'll never forgive me.'

I stand and brush the grit from my hands. 'The world's changed. That's what you told me. I think that maybe forgiveness is like change—it comes in small steps.'

She reaches out. I fold into her arms, and she holds me tight, stroking my head. Neurochip or neuron, it doesn't matter, I am weak with her scent and touch.

She steps back, still holding my shoulders. 'Go. Get it over with. I'll be in soon.'

The house is still, like the breath has been punched out of it. A low rising sun floods the kitchen with soft pink light. The breakfast table, normally the morning hub, is empty. I walk to the hall. A small triangular patch of light illuminates one wall, but darkness paints the rest. I step closer to the staircase and am startled to see Claire in the shadows, sitting on the landing, slumped against the banister. I climb the stairs and ease myself down next to her. She stares into space like I'm not there.

'Mom—'

'They might have saved you, you know?' Her voice is barely a whisper. 'If there are ever any charges—'

'Yes, they might have saved me in one way. But I would have lost myself in other ways that I couldn't live with. I did for them what they would have done for me.'

'Jenna,' she sighs.

'If it's a mistake, it's *my* mistake. Give me that.'

She tilts her head back, looking up, slightly rocking, like she is trying to sift the events out of herself.

He shakes his head without saying anything. Shaking it much too long, and a knot grows in my throat. 'You don't know the risks, Jenna,' he finally says. 'You just don't know the risks.'

I put my hand on his shoulder. 'Maybe I just know different risks than the ones you know.' He doesn't reply. 'I'm here today, the same as you,' I say. 'Isn't that enough?'

He is silent, but at least his head has stopped shaking. He finally reaches up and lays his hand on mine. Mother looks at me, her eyes focused once again, full of something that I am certain has no word or definition. Something the old Jenna never saw and something the new Jenna is only just understanding. She breathes in deeply and puts an arm around each of us. We are a tangled web of arms and tears, melting and holding. We sit in the dark cavern of stairs, giving ourselves time like we are a starfish regenerating an arm and learning how to move again.

Lily appears at the bottom of the stairs. She looks at Mother, her eyes hopeful, filled with the something that occupied Claire's just a moment ago. Mother lifts her gaze to meet Lily's, a long exchange in a language only they know. And finally Claire sighs and asks, 'Shall I put on a pot of coffee?'

A billion years of spinning. We are not immune to momentum.

Lily nods. 'I'll help you.'

We untangle ourselves and are just at the bottom of the stairs when there is a firm knock at the door.

'Who could that be this early?' Claire asks.

'It might be Simmons,' Father answers.

Or maybe someone else, I think. Maybe someone Allys told. Maybe someone who is here for me.

'I'll have to break the news that we don't need storage anymore,' Father says as he reaches for the door handle.

Should I warn them?

The door is already swinging open. Father's surprise is obvious, and he hesitates, not knowing the visitors.

Mother steps forward. 'Can we help you?'

'Are you the parents of Jenna Fox?'

Mother and Father exchange glances. I see Mother's body weight shift, like she will change into a wall if she needs to.

I step from the shadows. 'Yes, they are,' I say.

'We're Allys's parents, your daughter's schoolmate.'

'Yes?' Father says.

'We know about Jenna,' her father explains. 'Our daughter—' His voice cracks.

'Our daughter is dying,' Allys's mother continues. Her face is rigid. Frightening. I watch her swallow, her hands tight fists at her sides. '*Please,* can you help us?' Her rigid mask breaks and tears follow. Her sobs echo through the hall.

'Come in,' Mother says as she reaches out, putting her arm around Allys's mother. She holds the sobbing woman in a way that surprises me. Like she has known her for years. Like she understands everything about her.

'Let's go into my study,' Father says. 'We can talk in there.'

'We'll be a while,' Mother says to Lily over her shoulder. 'Will you bring the coffee in when it's ready?'

They slowly usher Allys's parents into Father's study and shut the door behind them.

Lily and I remain in the hallway, staring at the closed door.

'Here we go,' she finally says.

I shake my head. 'Allys wouldn't approve.'

Lily lets out a long breath. 'What did you say about change? Small steps? If the world changes, I suppose minds do, too. Sometimes it just takes time and perspective.'

Have my perspectives changed? Yes. But Allys? The world?

'I'm not so sure,' I say. 'But I suppose you're right about some perspectives. Just a few weeks ago, I thought you were a dickhead.'

She smiles, tired lines fanning out from her eyes in a way that seems like we are sitting at her kitchen counter and not three years and three thousand miles from who we were. She puts her arm around me. 'Come help me with the coffee. And if you don't tell your parents, I'll let you have some.'

Baptism

We walk through the church as though it is a day like any other. Lily dips her hand in the holy water, bends her knee and moves her hand like a musical note across her chest—she, on her way to discuss seeds and plants, and I, on my way to meet Ethan.

But it is not a day like any other. Something is different. Something that is small and common like a whisper, but monumental and rare at the same time. I stop in the crosshairs of the church and look upward to the cupola. I close my eyes and feel the cool, smell the mustiness of history, wood and walls, listen to the echoes of our shuffles and my memories. I breathe in the difference of being on this earth now and maybe not tomorrow, the precipitous edge of something new for me but as ancient as the beginning of time.

Lily's feet shuffle closer and I open my eyes to see her standing just inches from me. Her fingers are wet, freshly dipped in the holy water, and she raises them to my forehead. I close my eyes again and she whispers a prayer, her hand touching my forehead and then passing across my chest and shoulders.

'How can you know?' I ask.

'Some things aren't meant to be known. Only believed.'

A drop on my forehead. Hardly enough to feel. But still enough for Lily. And maybe enough for me. Washing away the old, believing in the new.

The world has changed. So have I.

Two Hundred and Sixty Years Later

I sit in the center of Mr Bender's garden. He has been gone for so many decades I have lost count. I live here now. I moved here forty years ago when Mother and Father's house burned down. They've been gone even longer than Mr Bender.

Father was wrong about the two or two hundred years I would live, but I'm not bitter. Faith and science, I have learned, are two sides of the same coin, separated by an expanse so small, but wide enough that one side can't see the other. They don't even know they're connected. Father and Lily were two sides of the same coin, I've decided, and maybe I am the space in between.

'Jenna?' I hear the call of the only person on the planet whom I can now truly call a peer. 'There you are,' she says. It is Allys. She does not hobble. Her words are not harsh. She is a happier Allys than the one I met so long ago. The new Allys. Twenty-two percent. Not that percentages really matter anymore. There are others like us now. The world is more accepting. We worked and traveled for many years to create awareness about people like us. But I am still the standard. The Jenna Standard, they sometimes call it. Ten percent is the minimum amount. But people change. And the world will change. Of that much I am certain.

Allys and I live together now. We are old women in the skin of teenagers. Another factor Father and his scientists didn't count on, that biochips would learn, grow, and mutate because somewhere in that ten percent was a hidden message: *survive.* The biochips made sure we would. How much longer? No one knows. But Bio Gel has been modified for future recipients so that no one lives beyond an 'acceptable and appropriate' time. In our old age, Allys and I giggle about being inappropriate. We laugh easier now about a lot of things.

'Kayla's home,' Allys calls from the edge of the garden.

'Send her out here.'

I had seventy good years with Ethan. It wasn't until long after he was gone that I was brave enough to arrange for Kayla. She has his coloring, wit, love of literature, and sometimes his temper. But she has my eyes. My breaths begin and end with her. But I know that one day, when Kayla is of a certain age, I will travel to Boston in winter and I will stay there, taking long walks and feeling the softness of cold snowflakes on my face once again, because no parent should outlive their child.

She bounds around the corner. 'Mommy!'

'Shhh,' I say, holding my fingers to my lips. She quiets, full of knowing and anticipation, her eyes wide and ready, and as I look into them—*every time I look into them*—I am reminded of Mother, Lily, and the something that it took Kayla for me to truly understand. 'Come here, Angel,' I whisper, and she tiptoes close and nestles beside me on the bench.

I reach into my pocket and a squadron of birds already flutter at our shoulders. I share my fistful of seed with Kayla and we hold out our offering. The birds are immediately on our arms and hands. A dozen or more. And each so light. *A few ounces at most.* They take up only a handful of space, and yet their touch fills me in immeasurable ways. A few miraculous ounces that leave me in awe. And today, like each time they have landed on my hand for the past two hundred years, I wonder at the weight of a sparrow.

Acknowledgments

Many thanks to Lisa Firke, Amy Butler Greenfield, Lisa Harkrader, Cynthia Lord, Amy McAuley, Marlene Perez, Laura Weiss, and Melissa Wyatt for countless suggestions and support. For multiple reads, critiques, and patience, I am deeply grateful to Catherine Atkins, Shirley Harazin, Amanda Jenkins, Jill Rubalcaba, and Nancy Werlin.

This book would not be finished without the encouragement and nagging of Karen and Ben Beiswenger. Even in the toughest of times you were looking forward and made me do the same. You two completely amaze me. Thank you to Jessica Pearson for on-the-spot advice and opinions, even as she was running out the door. Jess, just one more thing...

I am grateful to my spectacular agent, Rosemary Stimola, for her enthusiasm and boundless energy. She's as good as they come.

I could not have a more patient, encouraging, and smart editor than Kate Farrell. She knows exactly how to pull the best out of a writer and I am indebted to her.

Jessica and Karen, you inspired this book from start to finish. As Grandma always said, 'You've given me far more than I could ever give to you.'

And as always, my everything to my husband, soul mate, and partner in crime, Dennis Pearson. He makes it all happen. USA, baby, USA.

About the Author

MARY E PEARSON is the author of several books for teens, including *A Room on Lorelei Street, Scribbler of Dreams* and her latest novel *The Miles Between*. Her books have received many honors, including the Golden Kite Award, the JHunt Award for Young Adult Fiction, and the South Carolina Young Adult Book Award. *The Adoration of Jenna Fox* has sold translation rights all over the world and also feature-film rights to 20th Century Fox. It received a Golden Kite Honor Award, was a 2009 Andre Norton Award Finalist, and has been nominated as both a Kirkus Best Young Adult Book of 2008 and a 2009 ALA Best Book for Young Adults.

Mary writes full-time from her home in California, USA. She is married to the man of her dreams, has two lovely daughters and one terrific son-in-law, plus two very rambunctious golden retrievers. When she is not writing, Mary enjoys reading, working in her garden, cooking for friends and family, and traveling with her husband.

You can learn more about Mary and her books at http://www.marypearson.com, or find out her latest news on her blog at http://marypearson.livejournal.com.

WINNER OF THE 2008 GUARDIAN CHILDREN'S FICTION PRIZE
WINNER OF THE 2008 BOOKTRUST TEEN FICTION PRIZE

Todd Hewitt is the last boy in Prentisstown. But Prentisstown isn't like other towns. Everyone can hear everyone else's thoughts in a constant, overwhelming, never-ending Noise. There is no privacy. There are no secrets. Or are there? Just one month away from the birthday that will make him a man, Todd unexpectedly stumbles upon a spot of complete silence.

Which is impossible. Prentisstown has been lying to him. And now he's going to have to run…

Astonishingly powerful and breathtakingly exciting, *The Knife of Never Letting Go* is an unflinching novel about the dangerous choices of growing up.

"FURIOUSLY PACED, TERRIFYING, EXHILARATING AND HEARTBREAKING." SUNDAY TELEGRAPH

By Patrick Ness

Winner of the 2009 Children's Guardian Fiction Prize

Revered as a national hero ... married to the desirable Desmerelda ... cherished by the media ... soccer star Otello has it all. But a sensational club transfer sparks a media frenzy, and when he is wrongly implicated in a scandal, the footballer's life turns into a tragic spiral of destruction. South America's top sports journalist, Paul Faustino, witnesses the power of the media in making and breaking people's lives.

"In a vibrant modernisation of *Othello*, and with a strong South American setting, *Exposure* brilliantly explores the inequalities within society and the dangers of success." *The Guardian*

"...Stunningly good, blending *Othello* with Brazilian football, celebrity culture and the lives of slum children in a mix of brilliance and compassion." *The Times*

By Mal Peet

Winner of the Guardian Children's Fiction Prize 2002

During the long, hungry years of the Great Depression,
Harper Flute's family struggles to cope with life on the hot,
dusty land. Her younger brother Tin seeks refuge in the contrast of an ancient subterranean world. A world that nurtures
but – as disturbing events in the community reveal – can also
kill. A world that is silent, yet absorbs secrets. A world that
has the power to change lives for ever.

**"An irresistible and heart-rending tale... It is a novel you
can't leave alone while you are reading it, and one that
won't leave you afterwards."** *The Sunday Times*

**"Few novelists for young people deliver with such intensity
or so uncompromisingly... A deep, and deeply moving,
novel."** *The Guardian*

BY SONYA HARTNETT

At last, Miranda is the life of the party: all she
had to do was die. In the afterlife, she goes from
high-school stage wannabe to vixen vampire-princess
overnight. Meanwhile, Zachary, her reckless guardian
angel, goes undercover in a bid to save his girl's soul
before all hell arrives – quite literally – on their doorstep.

**Sink your teeth into a dangerous love story
played out in a dark eternal world where
vampires vie with angels.**

**"Suspenseful, entertaining, and enthusiastically
gruesome, Smith's latest will be lapped up
by vampire fans."** *The Horn Book*

By Cynthia Leitich Smith

A vibrant, deeply romantic and unmissable debut.

Seventeen-year-old Lennie Walker spends her
time tucked safely and happily in the shadow of
her fiery older sister, Bailey. But when Bailey dies abruptly,
Lennie is catapulted to centre stage of her own life and –
despite her non-existent history with boys – suddenly
finds herself struggling to balance two.
Toby was Bailey's boyfriend; his grief mirrors Lennie's
own. Joe is the new boy in town, with a nearly magical
grin. One boy takes Lennie out of her sorrow, the other
comforts her in it. But the two can't collide without
Lennie's world exploding...

By Jandy Nelson